A STUDY IN SHAME

LUCY SALISBURY

mischief

Mischief
An imprint of HarperCollins*Publishers*
77–85 Fulham Palace Road,
Hammersmith, London W6 8JB

www.mischiefbooks.com

A Paperback Original 2013

First published in Great Britain in ebook format by
HarperCollins*Publishers* 2012

A catalogue record for this book is
available from the British Library

ISBN-13: 9780007534791

Set in Sabon by FMG using Atomik ePublisher from Easypress

Find out more about HarperCollins and the environment at
www.harpercollins.co.uk/green

CONTENTS

CONTENTS

Chapter One

'Morrison, I have a confession to make.'

Morrison didn't answer, so I carried on. 'I'd like to suck your cock, Morrison. I'd like to crawl over to you on my hands and knees. I'd like to kiss your big furry balls, and then suck your cock, all the way.'

Still he didn't answer, but there was definitely something accusing about his stare, accusing and distinctly superior, like a bishop who's caught a choirboy pissing in the font.

I stuck my tongue out at him, then went on. 'Yes, of course I ought to be ashamed of myself. I *am* ashamed of myself. That's half the fun. Wouldn't it be nice, though, with your big black cock getting longer and thicker in my mouth as I knelt between your fat little legs? Longer and thicker, Morrison, until I couldn't take in any more. Yes, OK, I'd do it in the nude, if that's what you wanted, but wouldn't it be more fun to make me go the way dirty boys like it, with my blouse open and my bra pulled up to show you my tits? I bet you'd like that, and I'd feel so ashamed of myself, sucking your beautiful big cock with my tits out. I wish I could. I wish you had one, a huge one, long and thick and black. I'd suck so well, Morrison.'

I gave a soft moan as I lay back against the pillows. There was just time, if I was quick. My nightie came up under my arms and my hand went down the front of my panties to find the warm wet flesh of my sex. I was still staring into Morrison's eyes as I began to masturbate, imagining myself on my hands and knees with a really enormous cock in my mouth.

After a while I began to talk to him again, picking up where I'd left off. 'Oh, if only you had a cock. I promise I'd suck well, and I wouldn't be a tease. I'd let you do it in my mouth and I'd swallow for you. That would be shameful, so shameful, to have my tummy full of your come while we're in conference. They think I'm so prim and proper, such a good girl, such a nice girl, and all the time I'd have a bellyful of spunk.'

My eyes were closed and my back had begun to arch. I was going to make it, my fingers now busy in the wet slit of my sex, my mouth wide in a long sigh until I began to talk to him once more, with my fantasy growing ever more dirty as my orgasm grew closer.

'Wouldn't that be nice, Morrison, to have me suck you off? I'd pull out my titties and roll up my skirt. I'd pull down my panties and get dirty with myself while I sucked you, and when you'd done it in my mouth I'd swallow what you gave me. Only that wouldn't be all, would it, you big bad bear? There'd be more, lots more, in my hair and in my face, down my front and all over my tits and ... oh, Lucinda, you are such a dirty little tart. You ought to be ashamed of yourself, and I am ... oh so ashamed.'

I was, and it was wonderful, as always, the one thing that could be guaranteed to make an orgasm truly worthwhile. It didn't much matter what I was thinking about while I played with myself, as long as I knew I ought to be ashamed of what I was doing. Thinking about sucking Morrison off was not only shameful, it was also silly, which made it all the more delicious. There was a big smile on my face as I sank into the softness of my bed, my hand still down my panties as I enjoyed the luxury of a few seconds' more rest before opening my eyes again.

Morrison had fallen off the bed and now lay on the floor, the fixed stare of his beady red eyes directed at the ceiling, more accusing than ever. I picked him up and kissed his nose. Not for the first time I wondered what lunatic Chinese production manager had ordered a line of large, jet-black teddy bears to be fitted with red eyes. He looked demonic, but in a smug, disapproving sort of way, like a minor devil set to look over a group of damned souls guilty of some particularly embarrassing sin. I'd had to buy him.

It was 8.24 a.m. by my bedside clock, which left me fractionally over half-an-hour to shower, dry, dress, do my make-up and get myself down to the conference room looking immaculate. I could do it, just, maybe even snatch a coffee on the run, but breakfast just wasn't going to happen. Lunch was; that much could be guaranteed, because it said so in my schedule.

When I'd started nearly two years before, it had seemed the perfect job, PA to the CEO of a FTSE company, as it had been described to me. I'd been cherrypicked, straight from university, onto a salary far higher than I had been expecting and into a flat on the third-highest floor of our London headquarters. At the time, several people had gone to the trouble of pointing out that I didn't deserve the post, and that I'd never have got it if I hadn't been born with a silver spoon in my mouth. It was true, but that hadn't stopped me accepting.

I hadn't realised what I'd be sacrificing. At university I'd had plenty of friends and plenty of freedom. Now I had precious little of either, with barely a moment to spare for my old friends and no new ones. The girls on the main floor called me Posh Bit and I was very firmly not invited to share their social life. Nor was I meant to, as my contract clearly stated that I was to 'maintain rigorous standards of propriety at all times' and 'take scrupulous care not to engage in any activity which might risk bringing the company into disrepute'.

It was a philosophy my boss, Mr Scott, clearly believed in, behaving with Dickensian formality towards me, and if his eyes took a quick tour of my body as I stepped into the lift it was merely to ensure that I had presented myself to a standard appropriate to the company's standing. He even gave a little proprietorial nod when he'd finished, as if pleased with the quality of an acquisition. I returned a bland smile, hiding my true emotions, which were flickering between disdain and a need to be pushed down to my knees and held by my hair as he fed his cock into my mouth. He merely gave me his usual, very formal greeting.

'Miss Salisbury.'

'Mr Scott.'

'Do you have the presentation ready?'

'Yes, sir.'

As the lift descended he began to outline his strategy for the meeting, but I knew it already and only pretended to listen while allowing myself a little fantasy. He was big and dark, with a rough edge thinly concealed beneath the veneer of sophistication. Thirty, maybe forty years before, he'd have been the sort of boss who made me sit on his knee and fondled my bottom as I took dictation, maybe even made me go down on him under the desk, or, better still, made me go down on our clients in order to improve our chances of getting a contract. Not that I thought he would ever actually behave like that, and nor did I want him to, but a fantasy is a fantasy and it's easy to concentrate on the good bits and forget about the drawbacks.

He was still talking as we entered the conference room. A couple of the girls were laying out pens and paper on the table, a near-obsolete practice when everybody seemed to come loaded with gadgetry, but we were very traditional. Both hurried to finish and one, Stacey Atkinson, even apologised as she left, but the look she gave me was anything but contrite, more venomous. I gave her what I hoped was a sympathetic smile, although I knew it was hopeless. As far as they were concerned, I was the enemy, and there didn't seem to be anything I could do about it. Mr Scott didn't even notice, as he walked briskly to the head of the table and picked up the control for the huge screen at the far end of the room.

'They're very keen on efficiency, Miss Salisbury, so I want this to run smoothly. Every detail counts, right down to having the coffee ready next door at precisely eleven o'clock, while ...'

He carried on, but again I knew every detail of what had become a familiar routine. I had imagined the job would be challenging, but it was really just a matter of common sense and making sure everybody did what they were supposed to at the right time. A quarter-hour of bustle and polite greetings for the half-dozen Chinese businessmen who were our clients for the day and Mr Scott was firmly in command of proceedings, allowing my imagination to wander once more.

I'd often wondered how business meetings could be spiced up, simply by being a little less stuffy and a little more imaginative. It wouldn't even be necessary to dispense with the formality we set so much store by, and if it was always good business sense to keep your clients happy, then why not happier still? I could imagine how it would go, two hours of intense discussion as we hammered out the issues of rights to a vast Australian copper mine which no more than two or three people in the room had ever visited, and then Mr Scott would rise to his feet and indicate the door at the far end of the room as he addressed them in his old-fashioned BBC English. 'And now, gentlemen, if you'd care to come through into the refreshment area, tea and coffee are available, while Miss Salisbury will be very happy to provide oral sex.'

They'd all want a go. In fact, they'd consider it impolite to refuse. So in I'd go, to the discreet little cubicle set aside for the purpose, with a single comfortable chair and a mat on the floor for me to kneel on. They'd come in to me one by one, in strict order of precedence, all very polite and friendly, but without the slightest hesitation for what they were making me do as they pulled out their cocks and balls for the attention of my mouth.

At the beginning I'd be ever so smart, kneeling in my stockings and heels, my perfectly ironed jacket and skirt, my crisp blouse, perhaps with a couple of buttons undone to hint at my expensive underwear, but no more. The Chinese Chairman would be first, and he would ask politely if he could fondle my breasts as I sucked his cock. It would be unthinkable to refuse, and I'd know he meant bare, so my blouse would come open and my bra would come up, to allow him to paw my flesh and rub at my nipples as I gave him his blow job and swallowed what he did in my mouth.

The first of the two Vice-Chairmen would find me shame-faced and flustered, my boobs still out and my hair in disarray, but that would only make him keener. He'd want more as well, to rub his cock between my tits and have me lick his balls, and, again, I'd be too polite to refuse. The next man would be eager and clumsy, dirty too, tugging his cock into my mouth as I sucked, then pulling my head back at the last moment so that he could watch as he did his business in my open mouth before making me swallow.

By then I'd be too turned on to hold back, despite being bitterly ashamed of myself. I'd pull up my skirt and stick my hand down my knickers, fiddling with myself as I waited for the fourth man to come in. He'd take full advantage, not only making me suck his cock but then bending me over the chair to pull down my knickers and enter me from behind. I'd be more than willing, sticking my bottom up like a she-cat on heat and rubbing myself while he fucked me.

I'd come with him inside me, so by the time he'd finished I'd be left slumped over the chair, sticky with spunk and sweat, well used at both ends. That wouldn't stop the last two men from the Chinese delegation, the first delighted by the state I was in and making full use of my cunt and mouth, the second disgusted and merely tugging his cock off all over my bare bottom. That would leave all six clients entertained, but Mr Scott and the others from our company would take advantage of me, coming in and making me suck their cocks, fucking me, touching me how they pleased, before finishing off in my face or up my cunt. They'd leave me on my back, masturbating, and as the last man closed the door behind him he'd tell me I ought to be ashamed of myself for my behaviour. At that I'd come, just as the catering staff returned to clear up after lunch, so that they found me on the floor with my legs spread wide and my tits out, my face filthy with spunk and my fingers busy with my sticky cunt.

Just thinking about it was making me shake and I was

forced to prescribe myself a strong dose of reality in order to calm down, by paying attention to Mr Scott's presentation for a while. He was my boss, attractive after his fashion, and I do like fantasies of being under male control, but there was something about him that always brought me down to earth. I could never put my finger on it, but, where with most men the jump between fantasy and reality can come with a tugged-down zip, I couldn't see Mr Scott letting me do the tugging.

Nobody had noticed the state I was in, but I could feel the wet between my thighs and couldn't help but wonder if they could smell my excitement, which made me feel even more ashamed of myself and even more excited. I was going stir crazy, and I was going to have to do something about it, and soon.

Chapter Two

What I needed was cock, but the trouble with cock is that it comes attached to men, generally. Men talk, and in the case of company men there's nothing guaranteed to get them talking faster and in more lurid detail than the conquest of their boss's PA, which was how they were going to see the encounter. Several of them had asked me out, some of them very attractive, but I'd turned them all down. That had given me the reputation of a stuck-up ice-maiden who thought she was too good to be seen with the plebeians, but that wasn't it at all.

The truth was that I didn't dare accept, because I knew what would happen if I did. I'd let myself go, even if I spent the evening drinking nothing but mineral water, and the consequences would be disastrous. Maybe I'd find a man who could handle me, more likely not, but the chances of finding one who could keep his mouth shut about the way I behaved when I was turned on were close to zero. It had happened before, and just to think about it was enough to bring the blood to my cheeks and make my tummy go tight.

I'd come up to university full of excitement and anticipation, but also very naive. A childhood as the only daughter of the ambassador to an Arab state hadn't been much use as training for life as anything else. My education had been expensive and single-sex, finishing at a sixth-form institution so deep in the countryside that the sight of a man was unusual, while computer access was regulated with a vigour that made the average authoritarian regime look amateur. By the time I left I was an expert at cunnilingus, largely thanks to Juliette Fisher, and had never seen a naked man.

That didn't last long. Some of the young men at my college were truly beautiful: golden British youth in the first flush of manhood, muscular Americans obsessed with athletics and English girls, intriguingly dark city boys with yet more intriguing bulges in their trousers. I had one of the latter first, and had is definitely the word. He thought he was seducing me, a shy skinny virgin who wore print frocks and had hair down to her bum. So did I, but it never occurred to me that he'd want to call the shots. It never occurred to him that I'd want him to get me ready with the handle of my hairbrush, never mind offer to return the favour, let alone sit on his face to have my bottom licked. That was the sort of thing I was used to.

He wasn't, but I didn't even realise it was unusual for a man to call me a demented bitch as I lowered myself onto his erection with my sex lips spread so that he could watch as he took my virginity. I was enjoying myself too much, and he did have the most beautiful cock, long and thick and very, very black. He felt wonderful inside me, even better than the well-buttered courgette Juliette had used to break my hymen. On reflection, it might have been better not to tell him that, and it would certainly have been better not to tell him my Alabama plantation-owner fantasy while I was using his cock to rub myself off. In my defence, I must point out that he came so hard he splashed his own face, but suggesting he lick it up was probably another mistake.

I'd had a great time, and I was both hurt and surprised when he didn't want to carry on seeing me. Naturally, I knew that people can be sensitive about the colour of their skin, but he was fucking me at the time, and I wanted him to shame me, not the other way around. Most people don't see it that way, as I quickly discovered. In fact, most people won't allow a woman to fully express her sexuality without calling her a slut, even when they take full advantage, as I also discovered, and I didn't dare risk a repeat performance now that I was at work and in an even more enclosed and gossip-ridden environment.

The internet was out of the question, as my computer was part of the office network. It was monitored for 'inappropriate use', and, while that didn't cover the milder sort of dating and contact sites, I had no intention of allowing the company scandal-mongers to learn that I'd been surfing for sex, or even a long-term relationship with Mr Right. Not that I wanted anything of the sort, and I didn't even know who Mr Right would be, only that he wasn't the sort of man people would expect me to like. For one thing, he'd be quite rough, the sort of man who'd do things I found sexually humiliating without even realising it, and who didn't ask questions afterwards.

That was the point my thoughts had reached as I stood staring out of my window after work with a glass of wine in one hand and Morrison's paw in the other. Twenty-nine storeys up, the view was magnificent. The Thames seemed close enough to toss a pebble into, the cars moving through the rush-hour traffic like toys. I could see an immense amount of life, most of it very alien to me, especially the jumble of warehouses and industrial units along the margin of the river, even though the nearest was probably no more than ten minutes' walk from the front of the building.

It seemed to be some sort of depot, with big colourful lorries moving in and out, some being loaded or unloaded, others parked in a long single rank that backed onto the river. I could even make out the names, mostly continental firms, and see the drivers, talking together, lounging by their trailers with mugs of tea in their hands or seated in their cabs. They looked like the sort of men who'd do me good, big no-nonsense men who'd enjoy me without worrying about anything but the pleasure they could take in my body. It would be deliciously shameful too, and risky, bent down in the front seat of a lorry cab, my blouse open so that the driver could fondle my breasts while I sucked him off, and, if we got caught, well, I'd just have to suck his mates as well.

The thought sent a powerful shiver through my body, and again as I considered how easy it would be to make the fantasy into reality. All I had to do was make my way down to the street, stroll across to the depot, select my man and ask politely if I could suck his cock. He'd be surprised, but he'd accept and that would be that. In less than a quarter-of-an-hour I could have a nice fat penis swelling slowly to the motion of my lips and tongue while I played with myself down my knickers.

Life's never that simple. For a start, people would see me leave the building, so at the very least I'd have to take a roundabout route to reach the depot. Then there would almost certainly prove to be some nosy little security guard who wouldn't let me in, or if I did get in and summoned up the courage to approach a man he'd no doubt turn out to be faithfully married and would turn me down. That wasn't so bad though, because it would be deeply shameful to proposition somebody only to have him call me a slut and tell me to fuck off, and I could always have a second go.

Or he might turn out to have a weedy little cock. They say size doesn't matter, but a big well-formed cock is so much nicer than a small crooked one, just as a big well-formed man is so much nicer than a small crooked one. The problem is that you can't guarantee a big well-formed man will have a big well-formed cock, so I'd probably end up sucking on a little wonky willy, and even the humiliation of having to go through with it wouldn't make up for the lack of size. I'd just have to ask again. And there was another problem. They probably wouldn't believe my offer was genuine, or, if they did, they'd assume I wanted to be paid.

With that thought came a shock of humiliation far stronger than before. To ask a complete stranger if I could suck him off was bad enough, but to be offered money, and to take it, would be far more shameful. I wasn't going to be offered a lot, either, not by a truck driver. A man had once stopped me in the street and offered a thousand pounds for sex. I'd slapped his face so hard his glasses came off. A trucker wasn't going to offer a thousand pounds, maybe not even a hundred, certainly not for a blow job. Fifty? Twenty? Ten?

Every time I lowered my price I felt a fresh shiver of excitement. To suck a man off for money would be unbearably humiliating, but the mere thought of doing it for ten pounds had me close to tears. I wanted to do it, but I didn't dare. If I was found out I'd be sacked on the spot, and everybody was sure to find out. It was a great fantasy, but that was all.

Yet surely there was no harm in taking a walk down towards the river? It was a lovely evening and I could put on something pretty but casual, something that showed enough of my legs to intrigue any sex-starved men I happened to pass but which wouldn't raise an eyebrow from even the most censorious of my colleagues. After all, they all thought of me as a prude and would never, ever guess what was going on in my head.

'Well, Morrison, what do you think? Shall I sit in and have another glass of wine over an old film, or shall I go out and pretend to myself that I'm a tart?'

He didn't answer, which was good enough for me.

I pretended I was really going to do it, thinking the whole plan through and acting accordingly. The first thing was to dress the part, which was tricky. On the one hand I had to be able to get out of the building without arousing suspicion, but on the other I didn't want the drivers to automatically assume I was the stuck-up little bitch everybody seems to take me for just because I'm tall and blonde and speak decent English.

'What do you think, Morrison? How about my red dress with a hat but no knickers underneath? Yes, that feels right.'

It did: acceptable, yet daring, with intriguing possibilities.

'I do hope it isn't windy, that's all, because if it is my dress will blow up and everybody will see my bare bottom, and rather more. Wouldn't that be embarrassing?'

There was no wind, so I was quite safe, but the thought alone was embarrassing enough to add to the faint shaking of my fingers as I sorted out my dress and a pretty straw hat to go with it, an ensemble which would make it look as if I was going out on a casual dinner date. Next came my underwear and shoes.

'Do you think I should wear a bra? I'd better, I suppose, people are sure to notice with my nipples so hard, but let's make it something strapless. No stockings. My legs are smooth and I ought to show them off, while it's best to keep things simple. Flats or heels? Flats are more sensible, and there's less chance I'll be taller than the man who buys me, but tarts wear heels.'

I went for the heels, lipstick red to match my dress. Having a bra on but no knickers felt odd, and very dirty, leaving me nervous and excited as I looked myself over in the mirror. I looked cool, poised and perfectly respect-able for a woman of my age, but in my head I was a tart and a cheap tart at that, the sort of girl who'd suck a stranger's cock for a few pounds. Shades and a small red bag added the final touches and I was ready, but afraid to leave my flat and at the same time cross with myself because I knew perfectly well I didn't have the guts to go through with it and get what I really wanted.

In the end I had to force myself to leave, but nobody took the slightest notice. Nearly everybody had left anyway, and only Security even acknowledged me, with a polite remark as I signed out. I'd escaped, but I was sure I could feel their eyes on me as I crossed the plaza, watching me walk, curious at the way my dress fell against my skin without showing any evidence of under-wear, realising I had no knickers on and chuckling together over what that implied.

I felt good, for all my cowardice, naughty and free in a way I hadn't for a very long time. The evening was warm and still, but fresh from rain the night before. I knew there was a pub on the riverfront beyond the depot I wanted to pass, the Wharfingers, although I'd never been there. That provided my excuse and I was soon walking alongside a long high fence with the depot beyond. A sign told me that it was a bonded warehouse, which meant Customs and Excise, high security and no chance whatsoever of getting in without a good reason.

The discovery brought me both relief and regret but made it easier to enjoy my fantasy as I walked on. I was now opposite the row of parked lorries, and their drivers. Closer now, I could see that most of the lorries were French, Spanish or Italian, belonging to long-haul freight carriers specialising in wine and spirits. That meant they were a very long way indeed from their wives or girl-friends, and safely anonymous. Surely none of them would turn down the offer of a blow job and a grope?

I walked straight into the huge man who had stepped out from behind a parked van, bounced back, tripped over an uneven paving stone and sat down hard on my bottom with my skirt up around my hips and my bare fanny on show to the world. Not that the world was watching, but he was: a giant of a man with a red beard and a blue boiler suit, his face set in surprise but his eyes locked firmly on the neatly trimmed triangle of fur between my legs for the split second before I'd managed to cover myself up. Both of us began to stammer apologies and I could feel the blood rushing to my face as I pulled myself to my feet and hurried on, only to slow almost immediately, with a single thought raging in my head, painfully embarrassing and yet too thrilling to be ignored. He'd seen my cunt.

All I had to do was turn around and speak to him. I'd make a few light-hearted remarks, apologise for being so clumsy. He'd apologise in turn, again, assuring me it was all his fault. We'd get talking. Maybe he'd offer to buy me a drink, and all the while he'd know I had no knickers on under my dress. He had to react, to take me into the back of his van or one of the alleys that led between the old warehouses across the road, where he'd make me suck his cock or pull up my dress and fuck me up against the wall. Nobody would ever know.

I ran.

Chapter Three

Three large glasses of white wine later and I was wishing I hadn't.

'Oh, Lucinda, you are such a little coward.'

I'd said it aloud but nobody paid any attention to me. The pub had been crowded when I got there, so much so that I'd been forced to perch myself on the low brick wall that fronted the river, with one arm on the railings and one bottom cheek on the bricks. It was far from comfortable but I felt I deserved it, a punishment for being so pathetic. I'd held it in my hands, the perfect opportunity to get what I needed and I'd chickened out. He'd been huge, maybe six foot six, and solidly built as well. There was a good chance he had a cock to match, a massive pole of pale smooth flesh rising from a nest of gingery hair.

'You little idiot!'

A couple at the table nearest to me glanced across. She looked concerned. He looked amused. I gave them a frosty look, something I'm told comes naturally to me, and got up. The place was busy to say the least, with used plates and empty glasses everywhere, but I still took mine back to the bar and thanked the girl who'd served me. Polite behaviour was a habit drummed into me across the years until it was instinctive.

I didn't take the direct route back to the building, because it meant passing the depot and I couldn't bear the thought that the man might still be there and I knew I still didn't have the courage to ask for what I wanted, or even talk to him in the hope that he would take the lead. As I reached the top of the alley that led down to the pub, I could see straight down the road. He was still there, loading boxes into his van, two at a time, his massive shoulders working under his shirt.

'Go on, Lucinda, you can do it!'

At that moment a second man appeared from beyond the van, older, balding and carrying a clipboard. I gave up. Evidently it wasn't my evening. I crossed the road and started up an alley lined with little shops and restaurants, thinking all the while. He'd seen my cunt, a big rough man, a man like a Viking. That was another of my favourite fantasies, to be caught alone on a beach by Viking raiders. I'd imagine being picked up by the biggest

23

of them, slung over his shoulder like a sack of potatoes, carried on board their longship, stripped, fucked.

That was how the big man ought to have handled me. One peep between my legs and the outcome would have been decided. He'd have reached down, lifted me with the same ease he handled the boxes he'd been loading and put me over his shoulder with my bum in the air. I'd have struggled, just for form's sake, beating my fists on his back and telling him to put me down, calling him a beast and a bastard. His response would have been to flip up my dress and show off my knickerless bottom to the world, with my cunt showing between my thighs.

I'd have been dumped unceremoniously into the van, spread out on the floor with my legs apart. He'd have unzipped his boiler suit to pull out a truly massive set of balls and a monstrous cock, already half stiff. I'd have surrendered at the mere sight, taking him in my mouth as he straddled me. As I sucked he'd have pulled my dress up, taking my bra with it, to leave me spread naked beneath him in nothing but my bright-red heels and the dishevelled mess of my pretty clothes. Anybody who happened to pass would have been able to see, but I'd have kept my legs open, making a thoroughly rude show of myself.

When he was hard he'd have entered me, sliding easily in up my wet hole and making the show I was giving to the crowd now gathered in the street ruder still. My legs would be rolled up, my penetrated cunt stretched taut on the shaft of his massive cock as he pumped into me with his balls slapping between my well-spread bottom cheeks and the tight glistening hole of my anus exposed to the vulgar stares.

'That would be so nice.'

This time there was nobody to hear me talking to myself. The light was beginning to fade and there were only a few people about, with most of the shops shut. One wasn't, a curious-looking place with the single large window painted bright pink and decorated with a single word in gaudy gold paint – Harlot. It was a sex shop, the Pink Pussycat, and I found myself automatically quickening my step as I thought of dirty old men leering at pictures and videos of naked girls. Fifty yards on I stopped.

There was a café and I ordered a double espresso, sipping at the hot dark liquid as I pretended not to be looking at the door of the sex shop. An idea had occurred to me. I needed to make up for my cowardice. I even felt I needed to be punished in some shameful way. I badly needed to be naughty. What better way than forcing myself to go into the Pink Pussycat and purchase some embarrassing article?

I'd be safe, as long as nobody who knew me saw me go in or come out, and the chances had to be tiny. There was still a risk, but that was as exciting as it was frightening and it also stirred something rebellious within me. I had to do it.

'Go on, Lucinda, you little coward. It's the perfect punishment.'

It was, so horribly embarrassing that it would be sure to bring my already powerful arousal to the point at which I could no longer hold back. Maybe they'd have crotchless panties, cheaply made in scarlet nylon, the sort of tacky garment no decent woman would ever wear. I'd buy them, from an assistant who'd be trying to stifle his amusement and lust as he imagined me wearing them, my bottom no more than half covered by the hopelessly inadequate triangle of see-through red nylon at the back, the lips of my cunt peeping out from the slit at the front. He'd be some slick grubby-minded type, his head full of dirty thoughts as he eyed me up and down. Maybe he'd even proposition me, and I would turn him down, although the shame of it would be a wonderful addition to my punishment.

'Go on, Lucinda, just do it.'

I swallowed my coffee, spent a moment blinking my eyes and gasping for breath as I struggled to cope with the near-scalding liquid, and got up. There was a cash machine directly across the road, so I couldn't make excuses to myself about not using my card in the shop.

With the money in my bag I found the street empty for a hundred yards in either direction, so there was no way to back out by pretending I might be recognised either. It still took all my courage to walk those few short yards and push in through the door to the shop, but I did it.

'Can I help you, miss?'

She was small, tattooed and pierced, with startling green and blue hair like the plumage of some exotic bird, and as far from the image of the lecherous male I'd been imagining as it was possible to be. I could no more buy tarty knickers from her than from my own mother. There was no shortage of them though, three large stands festooned with the things, in dozens of designs and several colours, each labelled: saucy scarlet, bitch black, virgin white. I glanced around, desperate to find something, anything that didn't imply that I was after dirty, smutty sex.

'We've got some great deals on sex aids.'

'Oh.'

I walked across to the glass-fronted cabinet she was indicating. It seemed rude not to. Inside were some of the most grotesque objects I had ever seen, great bulky monstrosities made of hard black rubber and so large it was impossible to imagine them having any relevance to the human form at all. A neatly written sign in front of the three nearest informed me that they were butt plugs: the Butch, which I couldn't have got in my mouth, never mind up my bottom; the Bully, which would have made an elephant sit up and take notice; and the Bastard, which was quite simply insane. The names suggested they were designed for gay men, to my immense relief.

On the shelf below was a selection of vibrators, which were positively calming after the butt plugs. Most were ugly plastic things covered in embarrassing bumps and oddly shaped protrusions, but a few were stainless steel and really quite elegant, also reassuringly expensive. The assistant was looking at me hopefully and I realised I ought to say something, if only to find myself an excuse to leave.

'Do these come with a warranty? The steel ones.'

'Three years, but, believe me, they'll last you a lifetime. Let me show you.'

I stepped back in alarm, not at all sure what she meant, although it wouldn't have been the first time I'd been told to pull up my clothes to have a vibrator applied to my pussy. As it was, she merely unlocked the case, selected the largest of the stainless-steel ones, pushed the switch up to maximum and passed it to me. It was buzzing like a hive of angry bees and sent vibrations right up my arm, and further, making the muscles of my belly tighten. My reaction must have showed on my face, because she smiled and I found myself blushing hot as she took the vibrator back.

'Good, isn't it? But these are much cleverer. Just let me get it out of the harness.'

She ducked down to the lowest shelf, where there were several complicated harnesses made out of leather straps, each with a large dildo protruding from the front. I knew perfectly well what they were for, having had homemade versions used on me more than once, and found my blushes growing hotter still as she went on. 'It's a complete system; three sizes of vibrating dildo, harness, detachable cuffs, head harness and dildo gag, but you can buy the bits separately and the vibrators are the best. Here.'

She was holding it out to me, a vibrator made in the shape of a big black cock, very much like the one I imagined Morrison might have, complete with a pair of fat rubber balls. I took it, unable to control my shivering as my hand closed on the thick hard shaft, and then she turned it on. The vibrations were so strong I immediately let go and jumped back in surprise.

She laughed as she picked it up. 'It gets people like that. Or there's the thrust setting.'

An adjustment of the switch and the thing began to thrust in and out, a sight at once so obscene and so compelling that I found myself giggling nervously. I was going to have to buy it, because it was now going to be more embarrassing to make my excuses and leave than to go through with it, after the effort she'd made to be helpful. Besides, I desperately needed the awful thing applied to my cunt.

'How much is it?'

'Fifty-five, but it's a much better deal if you buy the whole system. Do you …'

She trailed off, but I knew she was asking me if I went with other women. I nodded, biting my lip, and she was smiling. Before I could stop myself I'd spoken the thoughts in my head: 'Do me.'

I sounded desperate, even to myself, but it had been a long time, too long. For one awful moment she didn't respond and I thought she was going to turn me down, only for her to speak again as she hurried for the door.

'Just quickly.' She locked the door and turned the sign to closed, then hurried back, grinning. 'Come on, in the back.'

I let her take my hand, numb with desire and with shame, the way I had been so many times before, willing but helpless. She was as bad as the rest of them, eager and dirty as she led me into a tiny storeroom that smelled of leather and sex. I let her kiss me, opening my mouth under hers after just an instant's resistance but quickly as urgent as she was. She'd slid a hand up my dress, following the length of my thighs to the top and groping for panties that weren't there. Her voice was a sigh as she broke away from my mouth. 'No knickers, bad girl. We know what you want, don't we? Let's do it over the desk.'

She pushed me down, among the litter of paper and pens and coffee mugs on the desk, my bottom pushed out towards her. I looked back, in time to see her lick her lips as she lifted my dress to get me bare behind before she began to wriggle herself into the strap-on harness, talking all the while. 'You've got such long legs, and such a little bum. I'm going to enjoy fucking you. What's your name?'

'Lu–Lucy.'

'Juicy Lucy, like the rubber doll. Perfect. I'm Charlie.'

'Pleased to meet you.'

'Stick it out a bit more.'

I stuck it out as requested, lifting my bottom to her as she fixed the huge black dildo into place. She gave me a slap, full across my cheeks and hard enough to make me gasp as she went on. 'You have such a pretty bottom. Even your bumhole's pink.'

'Thank you.'

She laughed, and put the head of the dildo to my cunt. I was soaking but it was still hard to take, stretching my pussy hole until I was open mouthed and gasping for breath. She'd got me, completely, bent over with my bottom stuck out and the fat black dildo pumping in my hole. My head was full of dirty thoughts, how I'd begged her for sex, how she'd told me off for not wearing any knickers, how she'd compared me to a rubber doll, how she'd slapped my bottom and told me I was pretty behind. All of it was exquisitely shameful, just the way I like it, and now I was being fucked over a desk in the rear of a back-street sex shop. Lost in ecstasy, I began to babble. 'Harder, Charlie.

Fuck me, fuck me harder. You can smack me too, if you want, anything … anything at all. I need it.'

'What you need is this.'

As she spoke she turned the vibrator on and jammed herself as deep in as she could get, squashing the fat rubbery balls to my cunt. I screamed, taken to the edge of orgasm in an instant, and over, with my fists hammering on the desk top and my heels drumming on the floor as I came to the sound of Charlie's happy laughter as she fucked me.

Chapter Four

'I am a dirty little bitch, aren't I, Morrison?'

He answered with his usual accusing, superior stare, which made me feel even dirtier. I pushed down the sheets and spread my legs, enjoying my nudity and exposure as I thought of what I'd done the night before. It hadn't been what I'd planned at all, but it had been extremely good. There was a tiny, niggling voice in the back of my head, telling me in a slightly despairing tone that I'd ended up having sex with another woman, again, but otherwise I was blissfully happy.

Charlie had handled me perfectly, not only taking control but humiliating me without even thinking about what she was doing. Then there had been the gloriously shame-filled moment of having to stay in position, with the dildo jammed up me as deep as it would go and the vibrator on full speed while she finished herself off by rubbing her cunt on the base. She'd been nice about it afterwards as well, which is always important, giving me a hug and a kiss before she opened up the shop again. Even the trip back to my flat had been exciting, with my guilty purchases concealed in a large plain bag, the full system, because after what she'd done to me I could hardly have gone for less.

Unfortunately, there was no time to bring myself to a leisurely climax over the memories of the night before. I'd just stripped off my nightie and knickers in anticipation of some fun when Mr Scott had called up to tell me I was to be in his office for a meeting at half-past eight. That barely left me enough time to dress, so I contented myself with a long moment with my thighs wide open and my back arched as I played with my breasts, wondering what he'd say if I came down in the nude, then got up.

At precisely eight thirty I knocked on his door.

'Come. Good morning, Miss Salisbury.'

'Good morning, Mr Scott.'

He had looked up as I spoke, and gave me a slightly quizzical look, as if there was something unusual about my appearance. As I had actually dressed, and made-up with my usual care, I knew there wasn't, but couldn't help but wonder if there was some sort of afterglow to good sex that showed. He adjusted the papers on his desk and turned to his computer, frowning at the screen as he spoke once more.

'This weekend is a team-building exercise, Miss Salisbury, as I'm sure you know?'

'Yes, sir. Bayford Woods. Rendezvous eleven o'clock in the main lobby.'

'That's right. As you also know, it's organised by Confidence. They've completed their analysis of staff-interaction patterns within the office and they have two recommendations. First, that we build respect for the authority structure by appointing team leaders with military ranks. Second, that we encourage internal competition and individual aspiration by playing a male team against a female team. This seems like a good idea to me.'

It seemed like a load of nonsense to me, but I knew better than to argue.

'Yes, sir, an excellent idea.'

'Good, because you'll be leading the women's team, with the rank of lieutenant.'

'I—I'm flattered that you should pick me, sir, but surely somebody more senior?'

I wasn't flattered. I was horrified. They all thought I was a stuck-up little bitch as it was, and trying to order them around during a paintball battle we were sure to lose really wasn't going to help. Then there was the mud, and the inevitable bruising, and at least thirty over-competitive young men for whom I was sure to be the prime target.

Mr Scott was shaking his head. 'Miss Phillips is in Antigua, Mrs Ryan's on maternity leave and Mrs Grierson feels such activities are incommensurate with her position as Chair. Look on it as an opportunity to show your authority and leadership skills.'

I was entirely in sympathy with Mrs Grierson and would cheerfully have swapped places with Miss Phillips, or even Mrs Ryan, but there was a hard edge to Mr Scott's voice and I knew full well that he felt I didn't make enough effort to be part of the team.

'Thank you, sir. I'll do my best.'

'One hundred and ten per cent, Miss Salisbury.'

I managed a smile.

That was only the start. I was not only expected to lead my colleagues on the coming Saturday, but also had to assemble my team, appoint sergeants and corporals, then outline our tactics, all on top of my usual workload. The only constructive thing I could think of was a remark my great-uncle Cyril had made about officer training during the Second World War. When asked how he would go about assembling a piece of complicated equipment in the field, he had replied, 'Sergeant, assemble the equipment', which was apparently the right answer. I decided to work on similar lines, by appointing the pushiest girls in the office as my NCOs and letting them get on with it while I stayed safely out of the way.

The obvious choice was Stacey Atkinson, a big dark-haired girl who was the number two in procurement. I'd heard she was from an army family, while there was something about her that frightened me and had led to more than one dirty fantasy. I called her into my office, told her she was my sergeant and ordered her to distribute a memo to all relevant female staff. She jumped at the suggestion, and that would have been that had not Mr Scott insisted on attending our meeting. That left me no choice but to exert my authority over the others, which left Stacey looking as if steam was about to start coming out of her ears.

I wanted to explain, but when I finally got the time I discovered that she'd already left, so there was nothing for it but to go up to my flat and collapse into a chair with a glass of wine. Feeling stressed and exhausted, I'd drunk half the bottle before I'd got dinner ready and finished the rest before it was dark. By then I'd started to perk up a bit, and went into my bedroom to examine my naughty purchase of the night before. It was an extraordinary piece of kit, and something I was going to have to keep very carefully hidden.

Charlie had put on the harness with the big black cock-shaped dildo attached in order to fuck me, but there was a lot more to it than that. There were two more dildos for starters, another one in the shape of a cock, equally long but thinner, which suggested it was designed to go up a girl's bottom, a very dirty thought indeed, and a third with two slim pegs, one above the other, and an extension below, made like two fingers and a thumb but very strangely shaped, which was positively bizarre.

The cuffs could be used separately, attached to each other, or fixed to the front or back of the harness. It seemed a bit odd to want to restrain the girl doing the fucking, until I realised that, if I'd had the cuffs on, Charlie could have fixed them to the harness while she fucked me, leaving me utterly helpless. They could also be fixed to the head harness, which was positively perverted, a sort of cage made of leather straps and designed to encase the wearer's head with her mouth either held open or plugged by the dildo gag, a double-ended monstrosity that made me shake just to hold it in my hands as I spread everything out on the bed.

Morrison was sat in his usual place at the top, his red eyes staring out from his furry black face with his usual supercilious expression. I felt I owed him an explanation.

'There's no need to be cross, Morrison. A girl's got to have some fun occasionally, after all. And besides, I didn't mean to buy all of this, just a vibrator. Not even that, really. I was going to get a pair of tarty panties and wear them as a punishment. You'd have approved of that, wouldn't you?'

His expression suggested that he would have, so I went on, picking up the head harness and fitting the dildo gag into place.

'And besides, it would be really horrid to have this used on me, wouldn't it? Look, these straps go around my head so that I have to take the short rubber cock in my mouth ...'

I shut up as I fed the fat black cock into my mouth. It was very thick, enough to make my jaw feel stretched, and there was no question that being made to wear it would feel like I was being punished, or a victim to some cruel bitch, Stacey Atkinson possibly, albeit a willing victim. I sucked for a while, then pulled it out. Morrison definitely looked as if he approved.

'You see? It's awful, and imagine how I'd be, on my back, with somebody sat on my face so that she can have her fun on the long rubber cock, maybe that bitch Stacey, wriggling her big fat bottom in my face and fucking herself.'

I broke off, imagining how Stacey would look, poised over my face, perhaps with four of her colleagues holding me down, her big muscular bottom stark naked. She'd be laughing as she lowered herself onto the long black cock-shaped dildo sticking up from my mouth, enjoying the look of horror on my face until she sat down and I was smothered between her meaty bum cheeks, with her anus pressed to my nose. It didn't bear thinking about, even though she was just the sort of girl I'd always gone for, but she didn't even like me.

'OK, maybe not Stacey. Charlie then. She's nice. No, you couldn't do it, you're a boy. No, Morrison, that's not fair. Besides, you don't even have the right equipment. Oh ...'

A very naughty idea indeed had occurred to me, something so deliciously dirty, shameful and downright perverse that for a moment I wasn't sure I could go through with it at all. Yet I knew how to deal with that sort of situation. A little time and a little more drink and I'd be ready. Besides, Morrison wasn't backing down.

'Well, I suppose so, if you really think I ought to be punished? You do. I thought you would. And I'm to wear the head harness with the gag in my mouth? You realise how stupid I'll look with seven inches of thick black cock sticking out from my mouth and another three inside, don't you? Yes, that's how big they are, it says so on the packet. You don't care? I deserve it? Oh, all right then, and I suppose you want me in the nude?'

He always wanted me in the nude. I'd been in the flat for over eighteen months but it still didn't feel like home and probably never would. That made going about with no clothes on feel vulnerable and exciting. The locked door and extensive security system meant that I couldn't actually have been much safer, but that didn't help my trembling as I stood to strip, slowly peeling off every last item of clothing until I was fully nude. Even in the bedroom being naked had its effect, but it was far stronger as I moved to the kitchen and made myself a large gin and tonic. The living-room curtains were still open and all I had to do was walk to the window and I've have been naked to half of London, but I was careful to stay out of view as I pulled them close.

Seated naked at the table I let my feelings rise, sipping my drink as I thought of how it had felt to be taken from behind by Charlie and wondering what was worse, that or what I was about to do. Both clearly came under the heading of inappropriate behaviour, but there was really no question of which would be considered more shocking, and that was the latter. Yet Morrison was right, I deserved what was coming to me.

He was waiting for me in the bedroom, his stare more censorious than ever.

'OK, OK, at least let me get ready. I know I need to be punished, but there's no need to be so stern with me.'

'No, not that one, Morrison. I may have been a naughty girl, but I don't deserve a cock up my bottom. Not the fingers either, for the same reason. You can give me a good fucking and be content with that.'

With the dildo in place he looked gloriously obscene, just as I'd imagined him so many times before, with a huge black cock and a set of heavy balls protruding from between his legs. A few adjustments and the harness was firmly attached, with the dildo on the thrust setting I needed to get my fucking. Next I had to put myself in bondage.

'Yes, I know I need to go in the wrist cuffs so you can hold me for my fucking. I'll have to put the head harness on first though, and after that I won't be able to talk to you, so you'll just have to do your business. Fuck me hard, Morrison. Really punish me.'

I picked up the head harness as I spoke, and slipped it on, taking the fat black rubber cock into my mouth and shutting myself up, which was a shame, because I love to talk dirty while I masturbate, but it had to be done. Now silent and shaking harder than ever, I strapped the wrist cuffs on and crawled into the exact centre of the bed, to kneel down with my face against the coverlet and my bum in the air.

Morrison was behind, ready to mount me, and as I picked him up the huge black dildo slid in up my cunt with embarrassing ease. Fixing my wrist cuffs to the harness was tricky, but I got it done and could still reach the control, which I flicked to maximum. Immediately the fat black cock was thrusting into me, deep and hard, with the vibrator running to send powerful shivers through my body and make me gasp every time the wrinkly rubber balls squashed to my clit. I was going to come almost immediately and there was nothing I could do to stop myself.

I struggled to focus, determined to get the best out of my orgasm as I thought of the state I was in, stark naked on my bed but for a cage of leather straps around my head that held a stubby black cock in my gaping mouth, my wrists strapped up tight behind my back with Morrison mounted on my upturned bottom. And he was fucking me, my own teddy bear, at last, his massive black cock thrusting in and out of my straining cunt and every touch of his balls to my clit bringing me closer and closer to an orgasm over which I had no control whatsoever.

When it hit me I'd have screamed the place down if I hadn't had my mouth plugged with the bulky dildo, and as it was I nearly bit through the thing. I couldn't stop it either, my muscles jerking uncontrollably as wave after wave of ecstasy ran through me, to the point at which I thought I was going to pass out before I finally rolled to one side and fell off the bed to land in a tangled, sweaty heap on my bedroom floor with Morrison's cock humping up and down in my bottom slit.

Chapter Five

'Lucinda Salisbury, you ought to be ashamed of yourself.'

I was, and it felt so good. In the space of two days I'd begged for sex from a shop girl, and got it, then put myself in bondage to be fucked by a giant black teddy bear. I'd woken to the memory of how utterly helpless I'd felt with my hands cuffed tight behind me and his huge cock pumping in my cunt. A few minutes later I'd come over the same dirty memory, spread out on my bed with my nightie up and knickers around my ankles. I'd been smiling ever since, and even the prospect of paintball didn't seem too daunting.

The leaflet from Confidence said to wear combat attire, an instruction repeated in Mr Scott's memo and my own.

I didn't have any, but I'd passed an army surplus shop on my way back after my encounter with Charlie and there was plenty of time to sort myself out. There was also the question of keeping the bruising to a minimum, because I knew I was going to get shot. Half the men in the office would be out to get me, while I always seem to end up on the loser's end in that sort of situation anyway.

Even that couldn't wipe the smile off my face as I set off across the plaza. If anything, the mild thrill of fear and the prospect of my certain and rather public humiliation was quite exciting. After all, if I couldn't be taken down to the main floor and put out for general use, at least I could provide them with the fun of paintballing me, and my reservations of the day before now seemed silly.

The shop was where I remembered it, and open, allowing me to purchase trousers, jacket and cap in a matching grey camouflage far smarter than the green or khaki. I added boots, thick socks and a heavy-duty sweat-shirt that would go some way to protecting my chest, and on sudden impulse a set of lieutenant's pips and a crimson plume to add a splash of colour without being too obvious. The mirror in the changing room showed a tall lean soldier girl, every inch the officer. With my hair up under my cap I looked better still, and while the jacket was a bit shape-less the trousers were really quite snug and set off my hips and bottom nicely. One thing was certain: I'd be the smartest woman in the team, at least at the start, and I decided to wear my new gear back to the building.

As I left the shop I was feeling more than a little pleased with myself, and enjoying a pleasant daydream in which I was being made to strip from my uniform on a vast parade ground with hundreds of people watching. I'd just got to the point at which my commanding officer was assuring me that my knickers really did have to come off along with the rest when a far more pleasant voice penetrated my conscience.

'Lucy? Lucy!?'

Only my father calls me Lucy, normally, and it took a moment to realise that the call was directed at me, which meant it could only be Charlie. She was across the road, her brilliant hair concealed beneath a hooded top, the girl who'd fucked me a couple of nights before. I was blushing as I went across, and slightly surprised by the expression of awe on her face. She'd been undoing the shutters of her shop, but stepped out into the street to greet me.

'Lucy? Are you army?'

The tone of her voice suggested she wanted me to be, quite badly, and I was tempted to lie, but thought better of it.

'Sorry, no. I'm going on a team-building exercise this afternoon.'

'Oh … you look great anyway!'

'Thank you.'

She walked around me, making little purring noises as she admired my outfit, and me beneath it. I could feel my blushes growing hotter for her very obvious attention, especially when she gave my bottom a gentle squeeze.

'Charlie, not in the street!'

'Sorry, but you look so good. Would you like to see me later?'

I hesitated, not sure if I dared accept and wanting to tell her that I wasn't a lesbian. After what had happened between us, it would have sounded ridiculous, but I knew better than to try to explain that the reason I found her attractive was that she made me feel ashamed of myself. I nodded.

'Maybe. I'd like to, but I'm not sure what time I'll be back.'

'I'll be here until nine.'

'I'll try. Must dash.'

It was a lie, as I had plenty of time, but she'd shaken me up. I'd made a date, with a girl, again. It was awkward to say the least, with my job, because, while the company was obliged to pay grudging lip service to same-sex relationships, associating with a girl who worked in a sex shop was another matter. I'd also been trying to put my past misbehaviour behind me, but I'd already failed at that, propositioning her within minutes of our first meeting. In any case, I hadn't had the heart to turn her down, and it was all too easy to remember how I'd felt bent over her desk with the thick black dildo pushing up inside me.

I'd hurried past her shop, which left me with no choice but to walk along the long straight road beside the bonded warehouse. There was a line of lorries beyond the fence, as before, with many of the drivers lounging nearby, although presumably different drivers. I deliberately turned my thoughts to the joys of big rough men, only to realise that there was a prime specimen right in front of me, my Viking giant.

He was standing outside what seemed to be a small warehouse and had already seen me, and recognised me. The blood went straight to my face and for the second time in a few minutes I found myself blushing over a previous encounter. I wanted to say something, an apology for the way I'd behaved, including leaving my knickers off, but there was no way of mentioning the incident without making matters worse. The most sensible thing to do seemed to be to smile and walk quickly past, but he spoke up as I approached him.

'Hello again.'

I already knew that his voice belied his appearance, while the sign above the warehouse suggested that he dealt in luxury spirits and might very well be the owner, a Magnus Brabant. Certainly the name suited him. I found myself smiling and slowing down.

'Hello.'

There was an awkward moment, both of us no doubt thinking of how I'd looked sat on the pavement with my legs apart and no panties on.

He was grinning as he went on. 'Sorry about the other day. I really should look where I'm going.'

'Not at all. It was my fault entirely.'

'No, really.'

It was going to be one of those very English conversations that consist entirely of exchanged apologies, but I knew what was on his mind and I had to say something. 'I don't normally go about like that.'

I'd said it, and I was instantly wondering why as the blood rushed to my cheeks. He at least had the decency to look slightly abashed, but he was still trying to hide a grin as he replied.

'It's quite all right if you do, not meaning to be rude. Look, I don't suppose you're free this evening? Perhaps you'd care for a drink, or dinner?'

My blushes hadn't got any cooler, because there was no mistaking the implication of what he was saying. He'd seen my bare pussy and he was keen to have another look, and no doubt more. I swallowed hard, struggling to sound calm and collected as I answered him in my best style. 'I'd be delighted, but unfortunately I'm busy today, until late. We have a team-building exercise, which is why I'm wearing combat gear, by the way. I don't usually dress like this.'

'It's very fetching. Another time perhaps?'

He was giving me the chance to back down gracefully, but I didn't want to take it.

'Yes, please. Tomorrow, for lunch maybe?'

'I'll book a table.'

That should have been that. I could have walked on, my date arranged, perhaps after exchanging a few polite remarks. Yet if he was as mild as his manners suggested any relationship between us was doomed to failure, while I very definitely did not want him to know anything more about me unless he was suitable. I opened my mouth to speak, knowing exactly what I wanted to say but unable to frame the words. He was starting to look puzzled and I was cursing myself for being such a little coward, but I finally managed to force myself to speak up. 'Thank you, but look, I …'

I stopped, then realised from the rising disappointment on his face that he thought I was about to change my mind. Suddenly I was babbling. 'I mean … I mean, it's silly, isn't it, all this flirting and messing about when we both know what we want? And it doesn't mean I wouldn't like you to take me out to lunch tomorrow, but … but wouldn't you like me to suck your cock, right now?'

My face must have been the colour of a ripe cherry and he was staring at me as if I'd gone mad. Yet I'd said it, breaking every rule of propriety by making a direct offer of sex to a man I fancied, and beneath my blazing embarrassment there was a lot of pride. He wasn't responding though, just gaping like a big red goldfish, so I took his hand and led him into the warehouse.

It would have been a bit awkward if the place had been full of employees, because, however naughty I was being, I'd never have had the nerve to suck him off in front of his staff, any more than he'd have allowed me to do it. Fortunately, it was a Saturday and he was alone, allowing me to lead him in among the stacks of pallets and loose cases to where a small office stood to one side.

Not a word was said. It didn't need to be, not now that we both knew what was about to happen, and what I was really like. There were several chairs and a small couch, onto which I pushed him down, then got on my knees on the rough industrial carpet. Still he didn't speak, perhaps realising that I needed to be on my knees, perhaps scared that he might break the spell.

As I reached for his fly, I was praying he had something worthwhile for my mouth, although I'd have done it anyway and the bulge in the front of his trousers was more than a little promising. Sure enough, as I drew his zip down I could feel the broad solid bulge of what had to be an impressively big cock in the white boxer shorts beneath. I couldn't help but purr as I burrowed in to pull it all free, his fat white cock and a huge pair of equally pale balls heavily grown with red hair.

My mouth came open. I allowed myself one exquisite

moment of shame-filled hesitation as I thought of what I was about to do, and then I'd taken him into my mouth. He gave a sharp grunt as I began to suck, with my tongue rubbing on the underside of his foreskin the way men like it best. Now there was no turning back, and no reason to be coy any more, with his cock swelling rapidly to the motion of my tongue and lips. I sat back, taking him in hand to masturbate him, my mouth curved into a sloppy smile as I broke the silence. 'Would you like to see my breasts? I think a girl ought to have her breasts bare when she sucks a man's cock, don't you?'

He gave a single urgent nod. I continued to play with his cock as I fumbled the buttons of my jacket open, releasing him only in order to shrug it down and off. My top followed, lifted over my boobs, bra and all, to leave myself bare to his gaze. His tongue flicked out to moisten his lips at the sight and I took him in hand again, stroking his balls and pulling at his shaft.

'There we are, titties out. Do you like them?'

Again he nodded, obviously not a great one for conversation, but his now stiff cock told me all I needed to know and it was turning me on to talk.

'I can see you do, and I bet you like my pussy too. Did you come over what you saw? I bet you did, tugging on your lovely big cock while you remembered how you saw my pussy in the street, how you saw my bare cunt.'

His cock was now a rigid pillar in my hand and he'd

responded to my words with a low groan. I'd sucked enough cocks to be fairly sure he'd come after another couple of minutes once I got sucking again and I wanted my own climax with my mouth still full. As I took him back in, I was fumbling my trousers open, to push them down along with the panties beneath, baring my bottom to his gaze and my cunt to my own eager fingers. I began to suck harder, and to masturbate as I did it, lost in bliss for the feel of having a really big cock in my mouth as I knelt on the floor in front of the man I was sucking, tits out and busy with my dirty little cunt.

We were going to make it together, my pussy already tightening as he began to push himself up and down to fuck my mouth. I took him deep, eager to swallow what he had to give me and go back to my colleagues with a bellyful of spunk, only for him to suddenly grab his shaft and my face, squeezing my cheeks together to force me to hold my mouth open as he pushed his cock down, aiming right at my face and jerking furiously hard on his shaft.

He came, an awful thing to do to a woman, holding her mouth open to deliberately spunk in it, and just the sort of thing I like. As jet after jet of thick white come erupted into my open mouth and over my nose and chin, I was coming myself, in a long sweet orgasm that lasted even beyond his, to leave me sitting back with my mouth wide open to show off the sticky pool on my tongue as I finished myself off.

Chapter Six

I thanked him afterwards, while he was trying to apologise for being so dirty with me, assuring him that I was fine and that he could definitely take me out on Sunday. There was still a reasonable amount of time to get to the office, so I made very sure I was decent before leaving him with a lingering kiss. As I walked away, it was hard to stop myself singing aloud. I'd now got two dates, while I'd more than made up for the cowardice I'd shown before. Much more than made up for it in fact, so much more that I knew I ought to be thoroughly ashamed of myself for my behaviour. A man had asked me out on a date, a polite well-educated man, and in response I'd offered to suck his cock, done it and then thanked him for holding my mouth open and spunking in it.

That was hardly ladylike behaviour, any more than his had been gentlemanly, which made me wonder what else he might have in store for me, a thought that kept the smile painted firmly on my face all the way back to the building. I was a few minutes early, but quite a few of my colleagues were already there, gathered around in little groups, men and women apart, laughing together or discussing their tactics. The men looked altogether too confident and too serious for my liking, each and every one of them in full camouflage gear, many with their own guns, helmets, goggles and other gear.

My own, female team weren't nearly as well turned out, mostly in clothes designed for look rather than function and very few with their own gear. Stacey was the exception, done up as if she was about to go into combat for real, and I made straight for where she was standing with her fellow NCOs. I was full of confidence after what had happened earlier, and determined to do my best to play my role, especially with Mr Scott lingering by the coffee machine in his reflective referee's vest. Stacey did a wonderful double take as she saw my uniform. I returned a salute and did my best to attempt a military manner as I addressed her. 'Sergeant Atkinson, are we all ready?'

'Er … yes, Miss Salisbury.'

'That's Lieutenant Salisbury to you, for today, or Ma'am will do.'

She gave me a filthy look, which I ignored as I carried on talking. 'We look like the weaker team, but I aim to take advantage of that. They're sure to push forward, probably leaving only a handful of people behind to guard their flag. That's why I'm going to keep nearly all of us back while only a few of us go forward, very wide, so that we can come around behind them. With any luck they'll be overconfident and easy to pick off, so that we can hold them at least until our forward group has managed to get through their defences to the flag. Any questions?'

Stacey raised a finger. 'With respect, Miss Salisbury … Lieutenant, you should let me do this.'

'What do you suggest then?'

'Your way, most of us will be bunched up in a group. They'll just rush us, coming in low and fast on all sides, so they'll take some hits but one or two are sure to get through. They'll have our flag before your forward group is anywhere near theirs. We'd be better off spreading out fast and finding cover from which we can pick them off as they come forward, with only two or three of us near our flag. That will slow the battle down, and we're smaller and more patient, which will leave us with superior numbers, and that's what's going to count.'

The other girls plainly agreed with her and I was tempted to tell them that they could go their own way and I'd go mine, but Mr Scott was listening to our conversation, along with two of the people from Confidence. When I answered, I was speaking for their ears more than Stacey's, knowing that I'd be expected to show leadership qualities. 'I'll take your advice on board, Sergeant Atkinson. Instead of sixteen back and four forward, we'll have eight back, eight spread out as you advise and four forward.'

I adapted my plan to include hers, showing not only leadership but flexibility, which I knew would go down well.

Stacey wasn't impressed. 'We'll be too thinly spread …'

'I'm in charge. That's how it's going to be.'

I turned away, making for our only team member from the post room, who was dressed in her work overalls and looked completely lost. As I passed Mr Scott, he gave me a nod of approval. I knew Stacey and her friends were going to be furious with me, even if we won, perhaps more than ever if we won, but they hated me anyway. I didn't even know the girl from the post room, and she obviously needed to be brought into the team, so I did my best to buck her up and let her sit next to me in the front of the minibus as we drove north.

The girls in the back were muttering together most of the way, but I ignored them, waiting until we'd reached the woods and been issued our guns and protective gear before ordering them to gather around. We'd been given pink paintballs, while the boys had blue. Stacey drew a bead on a tree and hit it from right across the car park, making my stomach tighten at the noise of the gun and the ball as it exploded to mark the tree with a broad pink splat.

I signalled her over. 'Sergeant Atkinson, you're in command of the base team. Both corporals are to be with the middle group, on either flank. I'll lead the forward team, although we'll be operating independently.'

Her face registered immediate disappointment and she was about to speak up, but thought better of it as Mr Scott approached. I made a show of choosing my three companions with care, all young athletic girls who could take care of themselves. Mr Scott rewarded me with another approving nod and walked off towards the male team, who were performing some sort of bonding exercise which involved clumping together as if they were in a rugby scrum and shouting a lot.

There were staff from both Confidence and the people who owned the site, one of whom told us to follow her to our base camp. As we walked, I quickly realised that the woods were far larger than I'd imagined, which probably meant Stacey was right and we would be too spread out, but I was sure that, if I changed my mind, I'd get marked down as indecisive. I'd also spotted a way to improve my personal chances of getting the flag, and greatly reduce my chances of getting shot. It was cheating, but that only mattered if I got caught.

My tension was rising fast as I gave the girls their orders at the base, once again ignoring Stacey's resentful scowl. With everybody knowing what they were supposed to do, I could only wait, with the seconds ticking by painfully slowly until at last the horn sounded and we were on our way. I ran immediately, down through big pine trees and across the path we'd walked along to reach the base. Beyond was thick undergrowth, then more trees and a barbed-wire fence that marked the boundary we were supposed to stay within. On the far side thick hedges ran to either side of a lane.

I shot a quick glance behind me to make absolutely sure I wasn't being watched, swung one leg over the fence, slipped on mud, lost my balance and went down hard, ripping my trousers on the wire. The material was still caught, but I could hear somebody in the woods behind me and wrenched myself free, to push through the hedge and tumble into the lane. I ducked down, breathing hard as I looked back, but it was difficult to see anything at all and if anybody had been there they weren't visible.

My trousers were torn from just below the waistband to halfway down one leg, a long jagged rent that left the side of my panties showing and made me wish I'd had the sense not to choose a pair decorated with little yellow ducks. Yet there was nothing to be done but tuck the piece of dangling cloth in and carry on as planned, running down the lane until I judged that I was beyond the male base. I could hear shouts and the occasional pop of paintball guns off among the woods, but the game only just seemed to be getting going.

I pushed back through the hedge and climbed the fence, more carefully this time, then started through the woods, ducked low. Just as I'd hoped, there was nobody about, and to judge by the noises of battle I was well behind the male base. I came close enough to the car park to see the vans, now with the battle hotting up nicely, judging by the distant pops and shouts, then angled into the woods, moving carefully from tree to tree until at last I came in sight of the men's rearguard.

It was fat Mr Potts from Accounts, a man whose eyes always seemed to be fixed to my bottom, so I shot him in his. He went up like a punctured balloon, taken completely by surprise, and I was past him before he realised who'd got him. Another man rose up from among a stand of ferns, his gun lifting to take aim squarely at my chest even as pink dye splashed across his stomach from my paintball, and I was diving for the flag, gripping it tight as I pulled it from the earth, screaming in triumph.

We'd won, or, at least, I had, and it was only the first game, but I couldn't help but feel extremely pleased with myself. I even took my jacket off and slung it over my shoulder in a deliberately casual style as I walked back to rejoin the other girls at our base. Unfortunately, things didn't seem to have gone too well. The flag was still where the staff had put it, and two of the girls were unmarked, but the rest were spattered with blue paint, most of them in several different places, while the men seemed to have found it amusing to aim for bottoms and breasts. Stacey was plastered, her front smeared with blue and the inside of one thigh marked with a double splat that was sure to have bruised the flesh beneath. I felt I ought to say something. 'Well done. You obviously put up a good defence.'

'No thanks to you, Lieutenant Salisbury.'

'We won, and that's what matters.'

'*You* won. We got sacrificed so you can look good in front of Mr Scott.'

'It wasn't like that ...'

One of her main cronies spoke up, then another.

'Bitch.'

'Arse kisser.'

I spread my hands in a gesture of what I hoped would be taken as an apology, but they weren't done with me.

Stacey stepped forward, the others following behind as she spoke. 'I say we get her, girls.'

Her paintball gun had come up, pointing right at my chest.

'Stacey!'

'You've had this coming to you a long time, Posh Bit. You get a count of five. Now run.'

'Stacey, you can't ...'

She could, and she was going to. I ran, terrified, dodging behind one pine and then a second, with her voice loud with triumph behind me, counting slowly down from five. At three, I heard the pop of a paintball gun and saw pink splash across a tree just next to me. A second caught my boot, a third my back and the air was full of laughter and the sound of their guns as they all opened fire together. Balls began to burst all around me, and against my body, on my arms and legs, my back and bottom, and on the bare flesh where my hip showed through my ripped trousers.

It can't have lasted more than a few seconds and I didn't even slow down, but I wasn't about to stop running, not for anything. When I got to a fence I went straight over, down a slippery bank and into the mud and water of the stream at the bottom, but even that didn't stop me. I could hear them behind me, and they were still firing, even though the balls were falling short, but it wasn't until I'd crossed a second fence into a field that I finally allowed myself to slow down.

My jacket was gone, and my cap, lost somewhere behind me. At some point I'd caught the rip in my trousers again, making the tear so wide it left half my panties and a good deal of my bottom on show. My skin was scratched and filthy, spotted with bruises and spattered with pink paint or slippery with sweat and mud; my hair was a filthy bedraggled mess and I could barely see through my goggles. I pulled them off and threw a last cautious glance towards the woods, but there was nobody in sight, only a cluster of large black and white cows at the far side of the field, so I sat down heavily in the long grass, only to discover that it concealed something squashy and unpleasantly warm.

Chapter Seven

I'd been shot by my own side. That sort of thing always seems to happen to me, and I've got used to it, but sitting down in a cowpat really was the final straw. I'd been meaning to tidy myself up and loop back to the car park, where I'd have been safe from Stacey and her pack of vindictive little bitches. That was now out of the question, with the seat of my panties in a state I didn't even like to think about and the rip in my trousers so wide I couldn't even cover up properly. My colleagues had camera phones, Stacey included, and I'd seen one of the Confidence people with a video recorder. I could not possibly go back until I'd cleaned myself up properly. That meant begging help from a local, but there was no other choice.

There were two possibilities, a big modern-looking farm at the bottom of the valley and what looked like a cottage set in a copse of trees, although only the red brick chimneys were visible, with a curl of smoke rising from one of them. I chose the cottage, not wanting to suffer the leers and jokes of farm workers, while with any luck it belonged to a well-off city couple who'd be sympathetic to my plight.

I was luckier still. The owner proved to be an elderly lady, plump, with a benign smile on a face like a wrinkly, rosy apple, who was working in her garden as I approached. I began to explain, but she took one look at the state I was in and began to tut and fuss, chiding me for my behaviour even as she offered all the help I needed.

'You poor thing. Still, if you will play these silly games, what can you expect? And you've torn your trousers. Really! Never mind, it's nothing a needle and thread won't fix. Now, let's get you out of those filthy clothes and into a hot bath. It's in the scullery, and you just need to leave the water running to make the boiler come on. Oh dear, have you had an accident?'

'I sat in a cowpat.'

She shook her head, as if I'd done it on purpose and it was further proof of my delinquency. I didn't bother to argue the point but just let her take over, not caring what she thought as long as she continued to mother me. She told me she was called Mrs Forbes, without adding a Christian name, which seemed to set the seal on our relationship, but that felt right, and I said my name was Lucy in case Lucinda made her think I was pretentious.

The bath in the scullery was a huge cast-iron thing standing on four squat legs. Mrs Forbes turned on the taps, then began to fiddle with a washing machine, talking all the while. 'Come along, out of your clothes. What a state you are in! And all this pink business! What is it, the dye they have in those paintballs, I imagine. Come along, you needn't be embarrassed in front of me, young lady.'

I made a face but began to strip, as she clearly had no intention of leaving the room. Not that it mattered, as she was utterly indifferent to my nudity but shocked by the state of my clothes, tutting and shaking her head as she inspected them, while I stood there stark naked waiting for the bath to fill up. She had the washing machine going before I could get in, but finally left. I closed the door behind her and climbed into the bath, slowly immersing my bruised and filthy body into the near-scalding water.

It was bliss, and as I settled into the bath I closed my eyes and let my mouth come open in a long contented sigh. She was still talking to me, or at least to herself, wondering if she had the right shade of grey thread in her sewing box to mend my trousers properly, but as I laid my head back to wash the mud out of my hair her voice was blocked out. When I came up again, she'd stopped talking and the only sound was the steady hum of the washing machine. I began to soap myself, wincing at the scratches and bruises, most of which were on my legs, but when it came to the paintball hits they'd mostly been aiming for my bottom and plenty of shots had gone home.

'Bitches!'

I meant it, but I was already fighting my reaction to what they'd done to me. They'd shot me, my own team, and even though there'd been nothing openly sexual about it I knew it would end up turning me on. So many of my fantasies involved having nasty things done to me by girls like Stacey and her friends; being made to strip for their amusement, having my face pushed in food or mud, being held down while they took it in turns to sit on my face. Being shot with paintballs came close, especially when I'd ended up muddy and bruised, with my clothes torn and my body filthy.

'Mrs Forbes?'

There was no answer, which presumably meant she'd gone back outside to carry on with her gardening. I let my hand slip between my legs, telling myself I needed a wash anyway and that a little rub of my clit wouldn't hurt. The first touch sent a shock of pleasure through me, surprisingly strong, and I pulled my hand away, telling myself I was not going to masturbate in Mrs Forbes' bath.

I turned my attention to my feet, trying hard not to think about my shameful fate and the girls who'd inflicted it on me. It wasn't easy, with my body spotted with bruises where their paintballs had got me, especially now that I was immersed in hot soapy water, while my endorphins had kicked in, combining to soothe my aches and pains. Every inch of my body felt sensitive, so that there was nowhere I could touch that didn't provoke a reaction, and as I ran the bar of soap up and down the length of my legs I was finding it ever harder not to turn my attention back to my sex.

'Mrs Forbes?'

Again there was no answer. I bit my lip, telling myself I needed to wash my bottom properly but knowing that to touch my bruised cheeks was sure to set me off again, never mind between them. Yet it had to be done, and I pulled my legs up, then decided that I might as well enjoy myself at least a little bit more and rolled over, sticking my wet bottom out from the surface of the water. I'd closed my eyes as I began to soap my hurt skin, allowing my fingers to trace out the individual bruises as I washed myself. They'd done a thorough job on me, at least a dozen hits, some right in the middle, so that if I'd had no trousers or panties on I'd have really been in trouble.

I was glad I had been covered, as I knew full well it wouldn't have been nice at all, but fantasy is fantasy and the idea of being made to run nude through the woods as they chased me was immensely appealing.

My fingers had slid between my cheeks, teasing my bottom hole as I imagined how it might have been. They'd have stripped me first, nude except for my boots and goggles, then given me my count of five as I fled in panic among the trees, naked and vulnerable. Stacey would have got me with her first shot, splattering my bottom with pink dye and making me yelp and jump. I'd have tripped, gone down in the leaves and mud. They'd have been on me, laughing at me, spreading me out in the dirt, Stacey squatting over my face, pushing down her combat trousers and the panties beneath to bare her full pale moon as the others cheered her on to make me lick her bottom.

I rolled over. My legs came wide, hung out to either side of the bath, spreading my cunt to my urgent fingers. All it needed was a few touches and I'd be there, and as I started to rub I was imagining my humiliation as Stacey spread her bottom cheeks in my face and demanded that I kiss her anus. I stuck one finger up my bottom, just to be dirty with myself, my back arched as my rubbing grew harder. I opened my eyes to help imagine my own horror, only to find myself staring not at Stacey's round pink bottom, but at Mrs Forbes' round pink face.

She was watching me through the window, her eyes wide and her mouth open in utter disgust at my behaviour. Then she was gone, no doubt to come round and give me a piece of her mind for playing with myself in her bath. I started to panic, splashing my hands in the water as a great wave of embarrassment welled up inside me and I was babbling stupidly as the door slammed and I heard her footsteps approaching.

'I'm sorry, Mrs Forbes, really sorry! I – I just … oh, God!'

The door pushed back and she was glaring down at me. I couldn't meet her eyes and hung my head. 'I'm sorry.'

'I should hope you are. Imagine doing that to yourself, you filthy little baggage!' Her face was set hard, and for one awful moment I really thought she was going to throw me out in the nude, but she carried on, far from sympathetic but very practical. 'Right, we'd better get you sorted out then, hadn't we? Get out of the bath.'

I obeyed, too numb to do anything else. As I rose from the water, she handed me a towel, which I wrapped around myself, to stand shame-faced by the door as she bent to inspect the washing machine, muttering all the while. 'It'll be a while yet. What's to be done with you then? I'll tell you what ought to be done with you, young lady. I ought to put you straight across my knee for a good old-fashioned, bare-bottom spanking.'

She left the room and I was left gaping after her. I

couldn't speak, my face and chest were crimson with blushes and I was shaking so badly I could barely hold my towel. There is nothing, but nothing, as humiliating as being spanked bare bottom across the knee. Plenty of punishments hurt more, and plenty are dirtier, but for pure erotic shame there is nothing to compare with lying across somebody's lap with your panties pulled well down as your bottom is smacked. Twice Juliette Fisher had spanked me across the knee, although she preferred to use implements. Both times it had left me in a puddle on the floor, but both times had been purely for fun. This was real.

I stood there like an idiot, burning with embarrassment and arousal, deeply ashamed of myself for what she'd seen and what I wanted, but desperately in need of exactly that. She had no idea what she'd done to me, and was plainly embarrassed herself, but she was cross too, really cross. I wondered if I dared ask for it, if I could somehow phrase my appeal in such a way that she didn't realise I was going to get off on my punishment, but I was sure she'd see through me immediately. Then she really would kick me out in the nude.

She'd begun to make tea, of all things, and with the kettle on she went to sit down on one of the kitchen chairs. Her knees were stuck out, just as if she was about to take a naughty girl across her lap, and I was mesmerised. All I had to do was bend down across her legs and I'd be in spanking position. She'd tell me to get up, not to be so silly, but she was the one who'd said I needed a spanking.

'Just do it, Lucinda.'

I'd spoken in a breathless whisper, but she heard, turning me a quizzical, disapproving look. My mouth came open again, but I couldn't speak for the lump now rising in my throat, and, really, nothing needed to be said. I let the towel drop to the floor, stepped across to where she was sitting and draped myself across her legs. She hadn't tried to stop me, and for a long, long moment of hideous embarrassment I just lay there with my bottom stuck in the air. Then she spoke up. 'Very well then, as you seem to have a conscience.'

Her arm came around my waist, tucking me in place across her lap. I braced my feet on the floor, a little way apart to keep myself steady, a position that left my cunt on show to the room. Her right knee came up a little, raising my bottom higher still and adding my bottom hole to the embarrassing display I was making of myself, but that was all the better, because it shouldn't matter what a naughty girl's showing behind while she's spanked. It did to me, adding fresh and beautiful agony to my shame, which hit a peak as she laid a hand across the cheeks of my naked bottom and spoke up. 'I'm not going to spank you hard, Lucy, but I am going to spank you well, for ten minutes by the kitchen clock.'

She lifted her hand, brought it down and delivered a

firm sharp slap to my bottom. My mouth came wide in a helpless gasp, not of pain, but of pure ecstasy. I was stark naked, laid across an old woman's knee as she spanked my bare bottom, and it was heaven. It stung too, even though she'd said she wouldn't do it hard, especially on my paintball bruises, enough to make me kick a little and wriggle my bottom in pain, stripping away any last vestige of dignity I might have retained by taking it well.

There was no mercy. The more I wriggled, the harder she spanked, until every slap was making my bottom cheeks bounce and spread to show off my bottom hole and cunt, with my legs kicking up and down and my hair tossing to the steady rhythm of my punishment. Soon I was getting hot, and she'd begun to smack me full across the tuck of my cheeks, sending a jolt of ecstasy to my sex with every blow. I could smell my own cunt, and I was sure she could too, adding yet one more dimension to my shame.

Then she began to talk. 'There's no need to be such a big baby about it, Lucy. You're only being spanked after all, and you know you deserve it, don't you? So come along, bottom up and try not to make such a fuss. Never mind what you're showing to me either. Believe me, I've seen girls' bare bottoms before, often when they're getting a spanking. You're no different, and certainly no better. Why, you big baby, you, there's no need to cry!'

I wasn't crying. I'd come.

Chapter Eight

She'd spanked me to orgasm, an experience that left me dizzy with reaction as I made my way back towards the woods a couple of hours later. Even without that exquisite peak, it would have been the most embarrassing experience of my life, and I couldn't get it out of my head. I'd been spanked. I'd been spanked bare bottom. I'd been spanked bare bottom across an old woman's knee. She'd made me come.

That was the rude bit, and I knew it would keep me on a high for days and leave me with an exquisite memory forever. To add to that I had a wonderful feeling of triumph, because if I hadn't had the courage to put myself across her knee it would never have happened and I'd have been left with the exciting but ultimately frustrating

74

experience of having been threatened with a spanking but not actually getting one.

The aftermath had been nearly as embarrassing as the spanking itself. I'd been hoping she'd make me stay nude with my red bottom on show until my clothes were ready, or even make me stand in the corner with my hands on my head to contemplate the consequences of my behaviour. Instead she'd wanted to know why I'd felt the need to be punished. She hadn't realised I'd come, and I could hardly have told her the truth if she had, so I was forced to tell her I believed in corporal punishment as the only effective way to atone for things I knew to be wrong but couldn't help doing, which was at least a half-truth. It also implied that I was hopelessly addicted to masturbation, which was the whole truth, and that I wanted to be cured of my dirty habit, which was an outright lie. Yet I couldn't help but wonder if I wasn't the only liar, and that she might have been just as keen to smack my bottom as I'd been to have it smacked.

I was smiling as I walked, now with my clothes clean and my trousers sewn up, but I had my worries. It had taken ages to get my clothes dry and the rip in my trousers mended, so long that if my colleagues had kept to schedule they'd have finished the exercise, packed up and gone home. That left me in the middle of nowhere with no money and no keys, which had been in the minibus with my other clothes. Not that I could imagine Mr Scott abandoning me and, sure enough, he was standing by his car, looking worried. I'd even found my cap and jacket by then, both marked with splashes of pink dye as evidence of what Stacey and her friends had done to me. His frown grew deeper as he saw me coming.

'Ah, Miss Salisbury. We have a bit of a disciplinary situation, don't we?'

My mind was still full of thoughts of spanking, and for one moment I thought he meant I was the one who was going to be disciplined, only to realise what he was talking about as he went on. 'I have already reprimanded Miss Atkinson, who I understand was the ringleader, and obviously their behaviour was wholly inappropriate ...'

I could see where he was going, preferring to avoid the scandal and trouble of the full-scale disciplinary hearing I was obviously entitled to, to say nothing of possible industrial tribunals if any of the girls were sacked. It was a bit rich, when I was sure that if he'd been the one they'd turned on all hell would have broken loose, but I knew which side my bread was buttered and was in no mood to play the bitch anyway. I interrupted him before he'd got into full stride. 'I think it would be best to drop the whole matter, for the good of the company.'

He stopped, clearly surprised, then rallied as he opened the car door for me. 'Well, I must say that I think that's the right choice, and, moreover, that you are showing a mature and well-considered attitude. Thank you, Miss Salisbury.'

As we set off, I was wondering how mature he'd have thought me if he'd seen me wriggling naked across Mrs Forbes' knee for my spanking, and whether he'd have enjoyed the view. He was always so formal, but then so was I.

***

By the time we got back, the day had begun to catch up with me. I was tired and hungry, but still determined to go on my date with Charlie. Mr Scott and I rode up together in the lift, our conversation strictly business, as it had been all the way from Hertfordshire. Only when I'd closed the door of my flat behind me did I finally relax, throwing my jacket and cap into the washing machine before pouring myself a very large glass of wine. Morrison was on the bed where I'd left him that morning, watching me with his disapproving stare.

'Yes I know, Morrison. I'm a disgrace, but don't worry, I've been spanked.'

I knew that wouldn't satisfy him. Nothing ever did, as he was a stuffed toy, but that was half the fun of it. He'd want to punish me himself, and I had one or two interesting ideas about what ought to be done with me, although that was going to have to wait.

'Yes, you're right. I enjoyed it far too much and I ought to be dealt with properly, certainly for sucking Magnus off, although I don't see why I should be given a punishment for being shot by my own side at paintball. Because it turned me on? Oh, all right, do what you want with me, you beastly bear!'

The wine was beginning to pick me up and I'd have done it then and there had I not needed to get ready for Charlie. I wasn't at all sure what she was expecting of the evening, expect that it was likely to involve sex, or, at least, I hoped it would. Another problem was what to wear. She'd liked my uniform, but my jacket and cap weren't going to be dry in time and even after Mrs Forbes has sewn up the rip in my trousers I'd have looked a bit of a ragamuffin.

In the end, I decided on one of my work suits, because if she liked one sort of uniform she might well like what was in effect another, while it made it easy to get in and out of the building. I was also hoping that if I dressed to the nines she might enjoy taking me down a peg or two, which was sure to be nice. With that in mind, I chose a set of luxurious silk underwear in pale cream, heavily decorated with lace and including a slip and a girdle to hold my stockings up. The stockings, a white blouse, a navy-blue skirt suit with a thin grey stripe, a matching bag and black heels completed my look, and if I was rather overdressed for a Saturday evening then at least that suited my prissy image.

It certainly didn't attract any undue attention, and I was soon at her shop and making a careful check of the street for people I knew before nipping inside. Charlie was at the counter, serving a plump middle-aged man with a bald patch at the back of his head who took one look at me and fled the shop.

'I hope I didn't lose you a customer?'

'Don't worry about it. He'd bought what he wanted and was trying to chat me up.'

'Oh. I suppose that must be a problem working here?'

She shrugged. 'Sometimes. I just tell them I prefer girls.'

'And do you?'

I'd asked because I wasn't sure, but she wasn't giving anything away. 'I prefer *you*. Shall we go down to the Wharfingers? I can lock up now.'

We waited until the shop was secure before resuming our conversation as we walked down the road.

'You look very smart. I thought you were going paintballing?'

'I changed.'

'Into an office suit?'

'I thought you might like it.'

'I do. How did the paintballing go?'

'I got a flag, but then I got shot by my own side.'

She laughed, making me blush, because she'd immediately picked up on my tone of voice and realised I'd really rather liked it, so I carried on. 'They were really nasty about it, and Stacey Atkinson, who I'd made my sergeant, was the worst of all. She gave me a count of five and told me to run, then shot me when she'd got to about three. The others joined in, all of them I think. I'd ripped my trousers so my knickers showed, and most of them aimed for my bottom. Most of them got me too. And I fell in a stream, and when I finally got away I accidentally sat down in a cowpat.'

'I wouldn't expect you to do it on purpose!'

I stuck my tongue out at her and continued. 'That wasn't the best bit ... I mean, the worst bit. I was covered in mud, and worse, so I went to a cottage. There was a very nice old lady there who washed my clothes and let me have a bath. Unfortunately I – I was playing with myself in the bath and she caught me.'

'No!'

'Yes, and she told me off. Then she spanked me.'

'Spanked you?'

Charlie's eyes were wide with excitement, but I could see she wasn't sure I was telling the truth.

'Seriously. When she caught me she said I needed a bare-bottom spanking. What was I supposed to do?'

'Not let her spank you, maybe? Seriously, Lucy, you let her spank you, bare?'

'I was already in the nude. I'd just got out of the bath.'

80

'Oh my, you lucky little bitch! Tell me about it, Lucy, everything.'

I knew what she wanted, and I was struggling not to giggle as I began again, sounding pathetically sorry for myself. 'She caught me playing with myself in the bath and she told me I needed … no, I remember, she told me she ought to put me across her knee for a good old-fashioned, bare-bottom spanking. That's what she said.'

'So you let her do it?'

Charlie's voice was a sigh, and I didn't want to disappoint her, so I carried on the story as it might have been. 'Not immediately. At first I thought she was just trying to make me feel embarrassed for what I'd done, but then she sat down on one of her kitchen chairs, with her legs stuck out, and she told me that if I had any decency at all I'd go over her knee and accept what was coming to me. I couldn't stop myself. I took my towel off and I bent over her knee. She took hold of me around my waist and stuck her knee up so I showed behind and she spanked me. She spanked me, Charlie, bare bottom, for ten minutes by the kitchen clock, and when she was done she made me do corner-time, you know, with my hands on my head and my red bottom on show to the room.'

She gave a long sigh and was going to say something else, but a group of people was coming the other way along the pavement. That broke the moment, but only briefly, and after that there was no question of what was going to happen between us. She was strongly turned on and I was no better, both of us touching and even risking the occasional kiss as we ate at the pub, sharing a bottle of wine while we waited for our orders and another over dinner. By the time we'd finished, I was pleasantly tipsy and it was dark, so I let her take my hand as we left the pub. It felt so good, to be led through the warmth of the night by a girl who'd already fucked me and now not only knew one of my darkest secrets, but also seemed to share it.

We were kissing the moment she'd got the shop door locked behind us, openly now, our tongues entwined and clasped tight in each other's arms. I let her lead, eager to be made to serve her however she wished, and as we settled onto the big red leather couch among the displays of sex aids and tacky underwear I was telling her how I liked it best. 'Put me over your knee, please, Charlie, with my blouse undone and my bra turned up. Turn up my skirt and pull down my panties while you tell me what a naughty girl I am, then spank me hard and put me on my knees to lick you, or, if you want to, you can sit on my face. I like that.'

'I bet you do, Juicy Lucy, but what about me? I want it too, and you're so tall and strong. I bet you spank really hard, and don't you want to get somebody back, after what Mrs Forbes did to you? Besides, I thought you said the bitches from your office shot you on the bum? Aren't you bruised? Come on, Lucy, spank me.'

I hesitated, a bit disappointed but intrigued. It always seems to be me who ends up on the receiving end, and it is what I like, but the temptation was there. I nodded as I decided to play her game. 'All right, you little slut, if that's your game, over you go!'

As I spoke, I grabbed hold of her, to turn her smartly across my knee. She squeaked in alarm, taken at least half by surprise, but didn't even pretend to resist, quickly wriggling into spanking position across my lap. I took hold of her around the waist, just as Mrs Forbes had done to me a few hours before, and as I pulled up the long loose skirt she was wearing to expose a fleshy little bottom well packed into see-through black panties I started to talk to her. 'One thing's for sure, Charlie, and that's that you deserve this spanking. Let's see now, for one thing you shouldn't call me after one of those revolting rubber sex dolls. Juicy Lucy indeed! And for another, I may have been knickerless under my dress the other day, but you appear to be wearing the stock, you bad girl!'

I began to spank her, slapping hard at her cheeks through the transparent nylon of her panties. She reacted with a deep sigh, sticking her bottom up to the blows and I began to smack harder, until her full cheeks were bouncing crazily with every slap and my palm had begun to sting. Obviously she could take it a lot harder than I could, but I wasn't about to let her off lightly.

'So it's like that, is it, you little slut? Right, let's have these silly panties down, shall we? Perhaps having a bare bottom will get it through to you. Down they come.'

She lifted her hips to make it easier for me to get her panties down and spread her legs a little, leaving the tarty black nylon stretched taut between her thighs, with the plump swell of her cunt lips plainly visible and her bottom hole a dark-brown star between her deeply cleft cheeks. In her position I'd have been burning with embarrassment, however much it turned me on, but she was merely having fun. Unfortunately for her, one of the stands nearby held a selection of leather spanking paddles, one of which I detached as I continued my lecture. 'OK, Charlie, if a bare-bottom spanking across my knee isn't enough for you, how about this?'

I brought the paddle down, full across the meat of her cheeky bottom, even as I tightened my grip on her waist. She gave a squeal of shock and a sudden violent kick, tearing her cheap panties so that they were flapping around one leg as I laid in, laughing as she struggled in my grip with her bottom dancing and her legs pumping up and down. Now it hurt, and I knew that every smack was likely to be repaid with interest once I was done with her.

Fifty seemed to be enough and I threw the paddle down and let go of her waist, expecting her to take her revenge on the instant.

Instead, she came into my arms, her entire body trembling violently as she clung onto me, her mouth seeking mine. I returned her kiss, but she broke away a moment later, to fumble my blouse open and pull up my bra to get at my breasts. She took one nipple into her mouth, then the other, but before I could relax into the pleasure of having my breasts suckled she'd moved lower still. I gave in to her need, lifting my bottom to tug up my skirt and quickly pushing down the panties beneath before spreading my thighs to her tongue. She began to lick.

Chapter Nine

The trouble with Charlie and me was that we were too alike. As I discovered while we talked together after sex, she loved to have rude things done to her, especially being spanked, tied up and just about anything that meant she got plenty of sexual attention. She also liked to dish it out, but not nearly as much, and even when she'd fucked me with the strap-on dildo she'd seen it more as a service she was giving me than as the cruel dirty act I'd been imagining.

I couldn't help but feel a little disappointed, although I tried not to show it, and she had given me a delicious orgasm under her tongue. She'd also been playing with herself while she was at it, and came before I did, so I hadn't even had the pleasure of having her sit on my

face, let alone the long slow spanking I'd been antici-
pating. I was still telling myself it had been a successful
evening as I walked back across the plaza, and there was
no doubt at all it had been a successful day. In fact, I'd
had as much sex in the space of 24 hours as in the
previous month, not counting masturbation, and a lot
more if you included the kinky stuff.

By the time I got up to my flat, I was having trouble
keeping my eyes open, and contented myself with peeling
off my clothes and flopping into bed naked. I wanted
to tease myself slowly to another orgasm over everything
that had happened, and lay back gently stroking my
cunt as I tried to focus. It felt good, but the sensation
was more soothing than sexy and the next thing I knew
I was lying face down, cuddled up to Morrison with
the morning light streaming in through chinks in the
curtains.

It took me a moment to remember that it was Sunday
and I didn't have to get up, then another to remember
my lunch date with Magnus and that I did, at least
eventually. It was nearly nine, which left three hours until
I was supposed to meet him at his warehouse, plenty of
time for an easy morning, and maybe a naughty one. I
got up, made coffee and showered, pausing by the bathroom mirror to inspect my bottom once I was dry. For
all the pain, Mrs Forbes had been as good as her word,
spanking me well, but not hard, yet my bottom still

looked as if somebody had been painting me to look like a Dalmatian and stained my skin.

Both my bottom cheeks and my upper thighs were spotted with paintball bruises, round blackish marks with pink centres. Each and every one of them smarted, with a dull ache I hadn't really noticed the day before with the excitement and the wine I'd been drinking with Charlie. There were an awful lot of them too, and for a moment I was reconsidering my decision not to have Stacey disciplined, before remembering that she and her friends had been shot too and that it was at least partly my fault.

I stayed naked as I padded back into the bedroom, addressing Morrison where I'd propped him against the pillows. 'Look at the state I'm in, Morrison. Isn't Stacey Atkinson a bitch?'

His expression suggested that *I* was the bitch and I'd got what I deserved, but that was Morrison all over. He was seldom, if ever, lenient with me, and I could see his point.

'OK, so I shouldn't have run off on my own and left them to their fate. Not that it would have made much difference, but yes, *mea culpa*. Still, you'd think she and her friends would have done a proper job of me, wouldn't you? I mean to say, shoot me, fine, but why give up so easily? If they'd caught me they could have held me down so Stacey could sit on my face to make me kiss her bottom hole. Now that would really have taught me a lesson.'

A shiver of pleasure ran through me at the thought, even though it was pure fantasy, and I carried on. 'It's not fair, is it? I didn't get my face sat on last night either. I thought I was going to, but it turns out Charlie prefers to get it herself. So I spanked her, hard, then let her lick my cunt. I suppose I'm going to get punished for that, aren't I?'

I was, without a shadow of doubt, but I wanted the experience to be deeply humiliating, and to cover everything I'd done, including whatever I got up to with Magnus after lunch. There was sure to be something, as we'd already broken the ice, and as I went to my cupboard I was once more congratulating myself for finding the courage to offer him the use of my mouth. Morrison was going to have to wait, but patience was another of his many virtues.

The day was as hot and sultry as the one before, while I was keen not to put any pressure on my bruises, so I chose another summer dress, blue this time, and once again went without panties. It felt even better than before, knowing that a man would uncover my little secret and no doubt take full advantage of my nudity. Even moving around the flat as I tidied up and completed my chores felt good, allowing my anticipation to rise gradually higher, until by the time I left the flat I was ready for fun.

Magnus was waiting for me, looking as huge as ever in smart jeans and a shirt, and as I reached him he lifted me clear off the ground to kiss me as easily as if I weighed nothing at all, once more sparking my fantasies of being thrown over his shoulder and carried off to be ravished. As he put me down, he was holding my bottom for an instant, and if he didn't seem to notice my automatic wince of pain he'd discovered something else. 'Don't you ever wear any knickers?'

'I might be wearing a thong, but no, I'm not. I've got no knickers, but there's a good reason ...'

For the fourth time I found myself explaining the state I was in and what Stacey and her friends had done to me. Magnus was sympathetic, but I could tell that he found the idea quietly appealing just as long as I was OK with it myself, so I assured him that I was. I even told him about my spanking from Mrs Forbes, which would normally have been too private for a man, but the idea of being put across his knee in turn was definitely appealing, at least once my bottom was better. What I didn't tell him about was my date with Charlie, not wanting to make him think I was a complete slut, although to judge by the expression on his face by the time I reached the end of my story he was hoping I was one.

'... so my bottom's too tender for panties, you see.'

'I'd like to, and we've just about time before lunch.'

He was indicating the door of his warehouse and I found myself smiling. Twice in a row I'd managed to turn a date on so much they had to have me before we ate, which was rather satisfying.

'Whatever must you think of me, Mr Brabant? I suppose you'll be picking me up over your shoulder and carrying me off to ravish me next?'

He didn't need telling twice. Before I could speak again, he'd ducked down to lift me up once more, this time with his massive arm around my thighs, and tip me up across his shoulder with my bum stuck high in the air, Viking style. I squeaked, trying to point out that we were in the street, but he quickly stepped into the warehouse. His spare hand immediately went to my dress, tugging it out from under his arm and turning it up to leave me bare bottom across his shoulder. No man does that to me and doesn't follow up on it, no man I fancy anyway. The moment he'd set me down in his office I was peeling off my dress. My bra followed, I kicked away my heels and I was in the nude, and turning to show off my hurt bottom.

'You see what they did to me?'

Magnus nodded and reached out to touch my bruised flesh, just gently. His hand was so huge his splayed fingers could take in my whole cheek, once more making me wonder how it would feel to be spanked by him, and then I found out. It was just a single gentle pat of admonition, the sort a man gives a woman to show interest, but it was too much for me. I stuck out my bottom, showing him everything as I spoke. 'Go on then, do it, spank me.'

He gave me another slap, making me wince as my bruises reacted, but I didn't want him to stop. Another and I bent down to rest my hands on my knees, making my position still more vulnerable and exposed, in the same rude position I'd once been made to hold to take the cane. He came close, to take me around my waist, holding me in place as he continued to spank me, his huge hand cupping almost my entire bottom as he laid in the smacks. I began to gasp and whimper, unable to hold back, and suddenly I was lifted clear of the ground and tucked under his arm.

My legs were kicking as he began to spank me in earnest. I was now utterly helpless, with the smacks of his palm on my flesh and my squeals of pain loud in the tiny office. It hurt like anything, and I could barely breathe, but I didn't care about that, only that a really big man was holding me up so easily and spanking my bare bottom. By the time he'd given me a couple of dozen smacks I was his, and he knew it. He dumped me on the couch, pulled out his cock and stuck it in my mouth. I sucked eagerly, desperate to get him hard and quickly successful.

I was rolled up and fucked, on my back with my legs around my ears and my smacked bottom thrust out as he pumped into me. It was far, far too long since I'd had a man's cock inside me and I went wild, clutching onto him and begging him to fuck me harder. He obliged, but stayed cool, handling me like a rag doll as he used me in different positions to get his full pleasure out of my body. First it was rolled up, then on my knees to take him from behind, and lifted onto his cock with one massive hand under my freshly smacked bottom, and straddled across his legs on the couch, then bending over, back in caning position with his hands clutching my hips as he thrust deep into me, faster and faster until at what must have been the last possible moment he whipped his cock free to spray come all over my upturned bottom cheeks.

Chapter Ten

That was only the start. My fucking left me in a state of drowsy pleasure, but I hadn't come and I knew my climax would be all the better for a little delay. We were also in danger of being late for lunch, which Magnus had booked at one of the good-quality restaurants that served the business district. He supplied their spirits, and as we ate he explained how his business worked, importing and distributing expensive brandies and whiskies, not only in London, but also in the US and Chinese markets. His clients included my own company, but I wasn't worried by the connection. However satisfyingly rude his behaviour in private, Magnus had all the credentials he needed to make him a suitable associate for me. Not even Mr Scott could have complained.

By the time we'd topped off the meal with a large glass of ancient Cognac, I was wondering if I dared take Magnus up to my flat. After being had on or over an assortment of couches and tables, I was beginning to feel that I deserved to be bedded properly, but, even with the elderly security guard who manned the doors on Sundays the only person likely to see us, I knew that the grapevine would soon be buzzing.

As we left the restaurant, I took hold of Magnus's hand and gave it a meaningful squeeze. 'I suppose you're going to take advantage of me now? At your place, preferably.'

'Yes, why not? I could lure you back to my house on the pretext of making you coffee, then seduce you.'

'That would be nice, and I bet you'd make me do all sorts of beastly things before you let me go?'

'I'd expect to get full value out of you, certainly. Who wouldn't?'

'I bet you'd even refuse to take me home unless I promised to suck you off in return for the lift? Men are such pigs that way.'

He nodded thoughtfully and I found myself with a happy smile on my face as we walked on. His car was parked in a narrow alley beside his warehouse, a big black thing with leather-upholstered seats that simply invited misbehaviour. It was also parked facing down the alley, which ended in a pair of securely locked gates and a high brick wall. He'd touched on one of my favourite fantasies and I didn't want to wait.

'You could always make me pay for my lift right now.'

'I could, and then I could be a real bastard by making you do it again later.'

'Yes, please. That's the way to treat me, and you don't need to be polite to me while I'm doing it either.'

He didn't need any further encouragement, but eased his zip down to pull out the full mass of his cock and balls. 'Right then, get your mouth around that, or you're going nowhere.'

'You pig! Take me home, right now!'

'Shut up and suck my cock.'

He'd taken me by the hair, pulling me down into his lap and rubbing my face against his cock and balls. I pretended to resist, but only for a second before my mouth had come wide to take in his lovely thick shaft. He kept his grip in my hair, moving my head up and down to fuck between my lips. I spread my thighs, inviting him to play with my cunt, and spoke again as soon as he let me up for air. 'I suppose you're going to want to molest me too, you bastard? I suppose you're going to make me get my tits out, and finger me, or touch my bottom up?'

'Yes. Get your dress up, you little bitch, let's see what you've got.'

I'd never have dared if I hadn't been so drunk and so

horny, but nobody could possibly see us unless they came down the alley and peered in at the car windows. I tugged off my bra, my dress came up and, in a sudden fit of daring, right off, leaving me in the nude but for my heels.

He approved. 'That's good. I like you stripped. Now get back down on my cock.'

I went, taking him in once more and playing with his balls as I sucked. His arm came around and under me, to cup my bottom. I stuck it out, eager for his touch, gasping on my mouthful as one big finger slid in up my cunt. He was now hard, his cock a massive column of pale flesh sticking out from his open trousers, so wonderfully virile I couldn't imagine anybody not wanting to suck it. I certainly couldn't resist, too weak to stop myself and keen to make my experience more shameful still as I briefly turned my attention to his balls, licking them as I masturbated him.

'I suppose you're going to do it in my mouth and make me swallow?'

'I'll do it where I like. Now shut up and suck.'

As he spoke he let his finger slip from my cunt, back a little, to push at the tight dimple of my anus. There was no mistaking the implication, that he'd like to put his cock up my bottom, not that I'd be able to take him, not easily, but it was a deliciously dirty thought. I stuck it out further still, now masturbating his cock towards my face as he teased my anus slowly open.

'No, not up there, Magnus, not up my bottom. You're too big, much too big ...'

I broke off with a gasp. He'd come, his cock erupting full in my face and soiling my hair, then in my mouth as I took him back in long enough to take what he had left and swallow before rolling over to spread my thighs, my fingers snatching for my cunt as I arched my back, showing off what he'd done in my face as I began to masturbate with his finger still well in up my bottom. It was perfect, nude in his car, my face and hair soiled with spunk, rubbing my dirty little cunt because I'm too much of a slut to control myself, already on the edge of orgasm, only for my ecstasy to break to the sound of my phone.

'Not now!'

He'd begun to play with my breasts, and ignored the phone, but I couldn't, my pleasure fading rapidly as it continued to ring.

'Oh, hell! I'm going to have to answer that, Magnus.'

'You just stay where you are.'

I found myself smiling as he extracted my phone from my bag. It was exactly the right way to treat me, to make me answer my phone while on my back with my legs apart, although he had at least been enough of a gentleman to take his finger out of my bottom hole, which was a pity. A glance at the phone showed that it was Mr Scott.

'Sir?'

'Ah, Miss Salisbury. Are you busy?'

I knew the answer to that one, but I had to put up some resistance. 'A little, not especially.'

'I need somebody to witness a document, several documents. Would you mind popping upstairs?'

'I'm, um ... not in the building at present, sir, but I'll come right away.'

I cut the connection, cursing softly as I pulled myself up in the seat. 'Damn! That was my boss, Mr Scott. Sorry, but I have to go.'

'No time to finish?'

'He's spoiled the moment.'

'I understand. Shall I wait for you?'

Yes ... no. I'll call you if I can get away, but I don't know how long I'll be.'

***

I was four hours, mainly because the documents related to the interminable divorce Mr Scott was going through with his second wife, a brassy woman who seemed determined to make everything as difficult as possible. She also took every opportunity she could find to put me down, which on this occasion included sending me on an errand to find a particular brand of cigarette. By the time I was finally free, Magnus had given up and gone home. He apologised and asked me out for the Tuesday evening, which was good but did nothing to reduce my frustration.

Mrs Scott's efforts to make me feel small had failed miserably, however much of my time she'd taken up, because both she and I knew full well that she only did it out of a sense of social inferiority. Besides, I'd found myself a new man, a really worthwhile man, and that would have been enough to shield me from a thousand of her sort. I just needed to come, while I'd also promised myself I'd wait until after my date with Magnus before indulging myself in another punishment from Morrison. Now was the time, and I stripped naked as soon as I was through the door, then flopped down on the bed beside him.

'I've been a bad girl, Morrison.'

He responded with his usual solemn, disapproving stare.

'I let a man take me out and get me drunk. In fact, I let him fuck me even before I'd had a drink. He did spank me, but I don't suppose that makes up for it, not really. No? I thought not. Then do you know what he did to me? He made me strip, in his car, and suck his cock in return for a lift. And he put his finger up my bottom, and I didn't mind. Now that, Morrison, was naughty.'

I could see he agreed. He always did.

'I know, I know. I need to be punished. How about a nice long spanking, like the one old Mrs Forbes gave me, over the knee and in the nude, or maybe dressed but with my skirt turned up and my panties pulled down to really make me feel my exposure. No? You want to fuck me? OK, if you think that's more appropriate, and maybe it's for the best, with my poor bottom so bruised. What, you want to fuck my bottom!? No, that's not fair, Morrison, not up my bottom!'

His cold hard eyes told me all that I needed to know. I bit my lip, imagining how I'd feel with a dildo driving deep in up my bottom hole. Just to touch the sensitive little star between my bottom cheeks felt delightfully dirty, even when I was washing, never mind what Magnus had done, but to submit to penetration would be stronger by far, about the rudest, most unladylike thing a girl could possibly do, and to be buggered by a bear. I had to do it.

'Oh all right, you horrible animal, you can do it up my bottom if you have to! I suppose it is the right punishment for what I let Magnus do, but at least have the decency to let me get myself ready.'

I bounced off the bed, happy and horny but still deeply ashamed of myself for what I was about to do. In fact, it was so shameful I needed Morrison to give me my orders.

'What shall I use then? No toothpaste, please, you know how it stings! Be kind to me, Morrison, because it's humiliating enough having to get my bottom ready for you as it is, without you wanting to hurt me too.

How about olive oil? That would be nice and soothing, but I suppose you're right. It'll get everywhere. Butter then? No it's not an easy option! I'd have to go into the kitchen, just the way I am, in the nude. I'd have to cut a piece of butter and stick it up my bottom to let it melt. And how do you think I'd feel about that, buttering my bottom hole for you? I'd be ever so humiliated.'

It was the right choice. I ran to the kitchen, my fingers shaking with need and with shame as I cut a cube of butter, stuck out my bottom and pressed it between my cheeks. It felt cold on my anal skin and at first it wouldn't go in, only to squeeze slowly up as my body heat began to melt it, a wonderfully dirty sensation. I was already in a state of bliss as I rubbed the butter well in and pushed a finger deep up my slippery hole, remembering how Magnus had done the same while I sucked on his beautiful cock.

I was wishing he'd taken me home and buggered me, or at least tried, because even allowing a man to attempt to put his cock up my bottom would have been deeply shameful, whether he succeeded or not. He was too big though, but then maybe, with a little practice, I'd be able to accommodate him. The thought of training myself to accept Magnus's cock up my bottom made me feel hornier still, but I forced myself to take it slowly, drawing out the agony of my own shame as I fixed Morrison into his harness. I'd been going to use the fingers, but I had to at least try the thickest of the dildos, and quickly had it fastened in place.

With Morrison sat against the pillows with his massive black rubber cock sticking up from between his chubby little thighs I crawled onto the bed, my well-buttered bottom stuck high as I took him in my mouth for a suck, licked at his balls and on a sudden shameful impulse kissed where his little furry anus would have been before pulling back.

'There, Morrison, isn't that a good way for a girl to say sorry, to kiss your bottom hole for you? Oh no, of course it's not enough, not nearly enough. Come on then, put me into my cuffs and that horrible head cage and you can bugger me. That will really teach me a lesson.'

I'd got everything ready, and quickly pulled on the cuffs and cage, filling my mouth with one stubby black cock as I prepared to take a second up my bottom. With my wrists cuffed together as before, I got down on all fours to lift Morrison onto my bottom with his monstrous cock resting between my cheeks as I clipped my wrists to his harness. Now I was really going to get it, kneeling and strapped up, my bottom well spread as I reached back to take hold of his cock, pressing the firm rounded head to my slippery, butter-smeared anus.

To my astonishment, it began to go in quite easily, but it was an overpowering sensation, tighter than a fuck and just plain wrong. Another push and I began to get tight, but I wasn't giving up and tried again, telling myself that it was supposed to be a punishment after all, and that Morrison certainly wouldn't let me off. I was sobbing on my dildo gag as I struggled to accommodate the mass of his cock, and then I'd done it, my ring stretching wide to take the fat rubber knob.

My mouth came wide with my bottom hole, until both were gaping. As my fingers found the switch, I turned the horrible thing on, and I'd have screamed if I hadn't been so well gagged, as all eight inches of thick rubber cock were jammed in up my straining anus. Now I was being buggered in earnest, the fat black cock pumping inside me to set me clutching at the coverlet and shaking my head in reaction, and not just to the sensation of having a prick up my bottom, but in pure beautiful shame.

It was only then that I realised why the instructions recommended the fingers for the best anal sex. The great rubbery balls were slapping on my empty cunt, a firm reminder that it was my bottom hole that was penetrated, but they weren't touching my clit. I began to squirm, right on the edge and desperate for friction, but it just wasn't going to happen in a kneeling position. More ashamed of myself than ever, I rolled over, to sit myself on top of Morrison, the dildo still pumping in and out of my bottom hole as I spread my cunt across one fat furry thigh and began to rub.

Chapter Eleven

It had been an extraordinary weekend, but that did nothing to improve the prospect of Monday morning. Mr Scott was sure to be in a bad mood, as he always was after seeing his wife, while unless I managed to avoid the office floor completely I was going to have to endure taunting and jokes from Stacey Atkinson and her friends. I was still sore as well, with my bottom and thighs now coloured with a dozen peculiar hues ranging from old gold to Imperial purple. Some of that was from the spanking Magnus had given me, and being buggered by Morrison, including faint marks on my wrists where I'd been pulling on the cuffs in order to get the dildo deeper still up my bottom.

I wanted to be very sure they didn't notice those, and

I was determined not to give them the satisfaction of seeing me react to what they'd done in any way at all. Fortunately, I had several pairs of tight running shorts, which I put on in place of panties, and an old-fashioned and extremely prim blouse with long cuffs that made me look as if I'd stepped out of some office movie from the eighties but successfully hid the marks on my wrists. I was still feeling jittery as I went down in the lift, and doing my usual thing of dreading reality while enjoying a fantasy about the very thing I feared. In this case, being made to show off my bruises by Stacey and her friends.

They'd corner me somewhere quiet, perhaps in the old print room, bend me over a photocopier and hold me in place while they turned up my skirt and pulled down my shorts to inspect my bottom. First they'd enjoy a good laugh over the state of my cheeks, before realising the bruises weren't all from their paintball hits. Stacey herself would have worked out that I'd been beaten and force me to admit what had happened by twisting my arm painfully tight behind my back. I'd admit to being spanked by Magnus, only to have my bottom cheeks pulled apart and my anus inspected too, after which I'd have to admit to anal sex as well. They'd laugh at me, spank me, stick a marker pen up my bottom and another in my cunt, at which I'd lose control and end up masturbating in front of them, spread out on the floor as I came over my own humiliation.

'Miss Salisbury? Lucinda?'

It was Stacey. I spun around, dropping the cup of coffee I'd been pouring for myself down the front of my skirt and all over the carpet. She gave me a surprised look and immediately bent down to help clear up the mess I'd made as I turned to the sink to try to do something about my skirt and to hide my blushes, apologising out of sheer habit. 'I'm sorry. I didn't see you there. I was, er … daydreaming.'

'Never mind, at least you can go upstairs to change your skirt. Look, Miss Salisbury … Lucinda, I want to say sorry myself. We went too far last Saturday, and it's really sweet of you not to take any action over what happened.'

She was holding out a memo, which I took. It was a formal warning about her behaviour, from Mr Scott himself, with an additional note to the effect that had it not been for my intervention she'd have been risking dismissal.

I smiled and shrugged. 'It's nothing, really. I probably deserved it.'

'No, you didn't. You were just trying to win, which is what it's supposed to be all about, isn't it? And it's not as if you owe us any favours. Friends?'

I found myself smiling stupidly as a great weight of stress I'd never really known was there began to drain away. She was holding her arms open and I went forward, to let her hug me and to return the hug. I could feel the strength of her arms and the size of her full firm breasts as they pushed against my own, so quickly kissed her and pulled away in case she somehow realised my instinctive reaction. Now she was smiling as she threw a quick glance towards the door, then pulled up the hem of her skirt.

'Look at this. That's from when they charged the flag. Mike Baker got me, after I'd got him, but the referee didn't take any notice at all! Then I got disqualified for tripping him up, but that was when we heard the horn go. You were brilliant!'

She was showing me a rounded bruise, much like the ones on my bottom and legs, but on her inner thigh, well above her knee.

Now I couldn't help smiling, although I very definitely was not going to start comparing bruises. I lied instead. 'I'm not too bad, actually. None of you got me from all that close to and I had thick undies on.'

'With yellow ducks on. We saw. Look, some of us are going for a drink tonight, would you like to come?'

* * *

I couldn't refuse, and I couldn't help but imagine that it was some sort of trick, which made for a classic fantasy. They'd take me to some perfectly ordinary pub or bar,

108

where I wouldn't be suspicious, get me drunk and then take me somewhere quiet to deal with me. I'd be stripped naked, my panties stuffed into my mouth to shut me up, tied up with my own stockings, my hands strapped tight behind my back and my ankles lashed together. It would all be on cameraphone, every awful detail as I was put across Stacey's knee and spanked until I was in danger of swallowing my panties in my pain and humiliation. Only when they'd got my bottom red and rosy would they let me up, by which time I'd be in a state of helpless arousal, allowing them to make me their plaything as I knelt naked on the dirty ground, licking eagerly at their pussies and between the cheeks of their bottoms. They'd film me as I kissed Stacey's anus, before spreading me out on the cobbles so that she could sit on my face to get her orgasm while I masturbated in front of them.

Of course, it was nothing like that, as I knew perfectly well it wouldn't be, just friendly banter over a few bottles of wine at one of the bars on the plaza. They did tease me, not in a nasty way at all, but joking about how gingerly I sat myself down in my chair and about my duck-patterned knickers, and they were no crueller to me than they were to each other. Inevitably, it got to me, but I knew full well they weren't like me and would be horrified at any suggestion of the sort of thing I'd have liked them to do with me, which was just as well as they were all from the company and anything more than a hug and kiss would have risked a breach of my terms and conditions.

None of them lived nearby, so they began to drift off one by one long before closing time and I was finally left to my own devices, sitting outside the bar with a nearly full glass in front of me and my head full of naughty fantasies. I wanted to play, and I couldn't help but wonder if Charlie was in, so instead of heading back for my building I made my way to her shop. The lights were out, and I knew she didn't live there, so I walked on, checking the Wharfingers before starting back along the side of the long fence opposite Magnus's warehouse.

The depot had about as many lorries in as during the day, despite the time, with powerful floodlights creating pools of deep shadow among the lorries, ideal to take me into and make me suck a few cocks. Unfortunately, the security was as good by night as by day, but as I passed the alley beside Magnus's warehouse I saw his car, parked exactly as it had been the afternoon before when I'd gone down on his cock. Evidently, he was working late, but I had no doubt he'd be able to find the time to give me what I needed and quickly crossed the road. A light showed high on the side of the alley, which was presumably an upper storey of his warehouse, although I hadn't explored it, but that was all.

I pulled out my phone, meaning to ring, but thought

better of it, because if the front door was open I'd be able to strip first and walk naked into his office as he worked over his accounts or whatever tedious task he was at, which was sure to be a nice surprise. That assumed he was alone, and if he wasn't the whole thing would simply be embarrassing and not in a nice way, so when I tried the door and found it was open I slipped quietly inside and stood listening as my eyes adapted to the dim light. I heard voices almost immediately, Magnus's bass rumble and another, also male but quieter, more diffident, and which I was sure I recognised. Puzzled, I shut the door and moved a little further into the warehouse. I heard Magnus's voice again, although it was impossible to make out the words, and the other, a single clear word. 'Please.'

Now I was sure, and my curiosity was simply too strong to allow me to go back. I could see reasonably well too, by the dirty yellow light coming through barred windows onto the alley and high in the front wall. The staircase was at the back and I moved cautiously towards it, and up, a step at a time. It gave onto an open floor stacked with boxes much like the one below, with a desk to one side and a big comfortable chair deliberately illuminated by a single lamp. In the chair sat Magnus, his massive legs splayed apart, his trousers undone to expose his genitals, just as he had for me, and in front of him, on his knees, his mouth full of thick white cock,

111

his eyes shut in ecstasy as he sucked, was my own boss, Mr Scott.

Neither heard my hastily stifled gasp of shock, both lost in the moment as one pleasured the other, and it didn't look like a mutually satisfying blow job; it looked like an act of worship. I could only stare as Mr Scott worked his lips slowly up and down Magnus's erection, which looked even bigger and thicker than when I'd been attending to it, desperately trying to get my emotions in order: envy, arousal, betrayal, a curious sense of pride and an urgent dirty need to crawl over and join my boss as he paid homage to Magnus's virility. If I'd thought for an instant I'd be welcome, I'd have done it, but I'd obviously disturbed a very private moment indeed, and when I finally managed to tear myself away it was to move carefully back down the stairs.

Outside in the street I let myself lean against the wall, my breathing ragged as I struggled to make sense of what I'd seen. I'd had no idea Mr Scott was gay, let alone Magnus, or, rather, bisexual, as Mr Scott had been married for twenty years and had grown-up children, while there had been nothing false about the way Magnus had handled me. Yet I could understand him wanting to suck Magnus off, out of sheer awe for his size and virility, even if he had no desire whatsoever for an emotional relationship with another man.

That made sense, or, at least, it was the only

explanation I was prepared to accept, but I still felt betrayed. After all, I was open-minded and Magnus could have told me. On the other hand, I hadn't told him about Charlie, which was really no different. In fact, it was exactly the same, which made it much easier to play down the negative side of my feelings as I started back towards the building.

Up in my flat, I was still too bemused even to play with Morrison, but had a quick shower, pulled on a fresh pair of knickers and a nightie, then collapsed into bed.

Only as I lay there in the darkness did my arousal slowly start to win through against my other emotions. I'd never seen a man suck another's cock before, and there was something immensely compelling about it. Mr Scott's face had been perfectly illuminated, as strong and as masculine as ever, and yet he'd had his mouth wide around Magnus's cock, a man stronger and more masculine still. I wondered how Mr Scott had felt, with his mouth agape around a cock presumably far bigger than his own. Sucking a man's cock had always been a dirty act to me and I'd have been deeply ashamed of myself, even though it would have been an essential part of my pleasure. Surely he should have been more ashamed still, to take another man's cock in his mouth and suck on it, feeling it start to swell, knowing he was giving pleasure he would normally have taken from a woman, and, worst of all, making another man come and swallowing down his spunk?

I couldn't stop myself. My hand had gone down my panties and I was fiddling with my cunt even as I used the other to tug my nightie up over my tits. I had to come, and not over the elaborate fantasies I'd had building up in my head all day, but over the memory of my boss sucking my boyfriend's cock. He'd been on his knees, just like I had, with his hand between his legs, just like I had. Presumably he'd been masturbating, although I hadn't been able to see his cock, and that was what tipped me over the edge, imagining one strong powerful man so overwhelmed by the sheer masculinity of another that he was prepared to go down on his knees and suck cock while he pulled on his own.

My back arched, my muscles started to contract and I was coming, with the image of what I'd seen fixed firmly in my head, and only as I subsided slowly into the softness of my sheets did I wonder how I was going to look Mr Scott in the eye the next morning, never mind Magnus when I met him for our date.

Chapter Twelve

What hadn't occurred to me at all at the time, but which I found more than a little irritating when it came to mind the next morning, was that Mr Scott was a hypocrite. He was the one responsible for the wording of my contract, and he was the one who was always stressing how important it was for me not to do anything that might tarnish the company image, as I told Morrison. 'And what does he do? He goes down on my boyfriend!'

Morrison did not approve, but then he very seldom approved of anything, unless it involved doing horrible things to me.

I went on, warming to my theme. 'And who knows how long it's been going on? All this time I've been playing Miss Goody-Two-Shoes – well, most of the time

– and all the while he's been indulging his gay fantasies! Do you think I should tell him I know, perhaps come to some sort of arrangement? Or do you think I should keep it in reserve in case he catches me misbehaving? No, that wouldn't be right, would it, but I don't want to admit I was peeping at them either? Oh dear!'

It was a serious dilemma, and not at all the sort of thing Morrison could help me with, when all he was really good at was adding to my feelings of shame and humiliation when I punished myself. At the thought of punishment, I realised that there was a possible way out.

'How about this? I'll tell Magnus and hope he's understanding, or if he's cross then maybe the offer of a chance to spank me for peeping will calm him down. That way we can work out what to say to Mr Scott together and I won't feel bad when I'm with him, because I don't really mind … or do I?'

I wasn't sure, because despite what I'd been up to with Charlie, and the fact that I'd wanted to crawl between Magnus's legs and join in with Mr Scott, I still felt jealous.

'Don't be a hypocrite, Lucinda. You're as bad as they are, and a dirty little Peeping Thomasina into the bargain. Maybe they should both spank me? That would really teach me a lesson, wouldn't it? And afterwards I'd have Magnus make Mr Scott promise to let me do as I pleased as long as I'm not too outrageous. How's that?'

For once, Morrison seemed to approve, but I knew I

was going to need a lot of courage and determination to pull it off, while there was every chance it might all go horribly wrong.

***

If there's one thing I'm good at, it's hiding my true feelings, and I managed to get through the day without doing anything to make Mr Scott suspicious. He was his usual self, and equally good at dissembling, which I suppose is a very British thing. As he closed our Chinese deal, he looked the epitome of the powerful and successful businessman, and not at all the sort of man who'd enjoy going down on his knees to suck cock, just as I must have looked the perfect English PA beside him, and not at all the sort of girl who gets off on her own humiliation.

Underneath it all I was growing increasingly nervous at the thought of my meeting with Magnus. I had to tell him what I'd done, and there seemed to be a very real chance that he would react badly, because for all the lip service paid to tolerance and equality there's still a strong stigma attached to homosexuality. Then there was the matter of sneaking into his warehouse and peeping at him. Yet there was one consolation, I told myself as I showered and changed into the red dress I'd worn when we first met: his reaction would be the mark of him as a man, and if he was violent or aggressive it was better to find out sooner rather than later. With that in mind, I didn't waste any time, but suggested a drink at the Wharfingers as soon as we met, then found a place on the wall where we wouldn't be overheard.

I forced myself to broach the subject as soon as I'd finished my first glass. 'I have a confession to make, Magnus.'

'Something naughty, I hope?'

'Yes, but you may not like it.'

'Go ahead. I'll try to cope.'

He looked concerned, and could obviously tell I was serious.

I swallowed half of the large glass of wine he'd just bought me and launched in. 'I went out for a drink last night and I was walking back this way. I saw your car in the alley and thought you might like to see me if you were working late. I went into the warehouse and I saw you with Mr Scott.'

Now he really looked concerned. 'You saw me with David Scott?'

'Yes. I'm sorry. Please don't be angry.'

He didn't answer immediately, and I could see that he was wondering exactly what I'd seen.

I told him. 'Everything. Well, enough anyway.'

'And you're not angry?'

'Me? No. I thought you might be. Why should I be angry?'

'Because ... you and I?'

He made a vague gesture between us and I found myself smiling.

'I was a bit jealous, that's all, but mainly I feel bad for peeping at you.'

'Jealous? Most women would be furious!'

'I'm not most women.'

'I'm beginning to realise that. So you really don't mind? Be honest.'

I drew my breath in, swallowed the rest of my wine and let go. 'I am a bit jealous and I wish you'd told me, but I don't mind. I don't mind because I'm the same. Bisexual. In fact, I'm seeing somebody at the moment, a girl from one of the local shops.'

'May I ask which?'

Now I was blushing. 'The Pink Pussycat.'

'Charlie or Emma?'

'Charlie. Do you know her?'

'She's on the local ratepayers' committee and so am I. I was in there this afternoon too, buying you a present.'

'And you don't mind?'

'Not in the least. Is there any man who doesn't like the thought of two women together?'

'Plenty, I'd have thought, and there are plenty of women who like the thought of two men together. But what about Mr Scott?'

'Ah, that is a bit of a problem. It's not something he's

comfortable with, and it's very private, while there's also the issue of his divorce.'

'I can imagine. I've met his wife.'

'Exactly, so it needs to stay a secret, and I'd probably better not tell him you know.'

'If you think that's best, and I promise not to tell anybody. But how did you two get together?'

'As you know, I supply your company. David has a private account and a taste for fine malt whisky. I run tastings occasionally, which tend to be fairly merry affairs, and, not to put too fine a point on it, I know a cocksucker when I see one. Sorry.'

I was blushing again, because he obviously meant me as well as Mr Scott.

'That's OK. I suppose a lot of people want to. Suck you, that is.'

He shrugged, but I wanted more and carried on. 'I wanted to the first time I saw you, and gay men I can understand, but somebody like Mr Scott? What does he get out of it? Doesn't it make him feel less of a man?'

'That's exactly what he likes, as do a lot of other powerful men. He spends all day making decisions, often ones that have a major effect on other people's lives. Taking a feminine role to another man helps him relax.'

'But he enjoys it, for its own sake? He certainly looked as if he was. For me it would be pure shame, maybe penance too.'

'You like that, don't you?'

'To be punished? Yes. Speaking of which, what happens to Peeping Thomasinas?'

'In this case? They get presents. I saw the position you adopted when I spanked you, Lucinda.'

'What do you mean?'

He laughed and lifted his glass to his lips, draining the contents in one, then stood up. 'You'll see.'

I'd already guessed, because the position I'd adopted, with my hands on my knees and my bottom pushed out, was the one I'd been made to get into on the sole occasion I'd been given the cane. There were canes in Charlie's shop too, long thin nasty-looking things with crook handles, just right for applying to naughty girls' bottoms. Magnus had seen the position I'd got into and he'd realised the implications, but he had no idea of the background to my caning, or how much it had hurt. And there was another problem.

'It's a cane, isn't it? I'm still a bit bruised.'

'Yes, it's a cane, and I think you deserve it, but we can wait, if you prefer?'

I closed my eyes, thinking back to how I'd felt, first told I was to be caned, then marched up to Juliette Fisher's bedsit. She made me bend over, in front of two friends, turned up my skirt and pulled my knickers down. I'd held my position while she enjoyed a long slow feel of my bare bottom and her friends enjoyed the view, all

121

the while holding the cane I was about to be beaten with in my teeth. Only when she was good and ready did she take it, to lay it gently across my bottom, swish it through the air, lay it across my bottom again and swish it through the air again before taking aim one last time, then lifting it and bringing it down hard across my cheeks. When I'd finally stopped jumping up and down like a mad kangaroo and let go of my burning bottom, she'd told me I'd get the remaining five the following week. It had been agony, every day, every hour, every minute filled with shame and apprehension, until I could think of nothing but my coming beating, and had masturbated myself sore.

'Give me one stroke now please, then tell me how many I've got coming to me and when you're going to give me them.'

He laughed. 'Do you know that David Scott thinks you're an innocent?'

I shrugged and took his hand, to allow him to lead me from the pub and back towards the warehouse. It felt strange, detached, with normal life going on all around me when I was about to be put into a situation that would horrify most people. Certainly I couldn't imagine any of the lorry drivers in the depot wanting to cane me, even though each and every one would prob-ably have enjoyed making me suck his cock and made full use of my cunt once he'd got me horny. This was different, something very English and perfectly suited to my sexuality, while Magnus was just the man to do it.

He held the warehouse door for me and spoke up as he locked it behind us, looking full into my eyes. 'That should keep any nosy little brats out, don't you think?'

I hung my head in shame and submission, following as he went into his office. On the table was a long parcel of black paper decorated with little silver stars, wide at one end and tapering to a point, a shape which would have made me instantly suspicious even if I hadn't already known what was inside. He passed it to me and I fumbled the wrapping open, to pull out a long brown school cane with a crook handle, exactly as I'd been expecting and virtually identical to the one Juliette Fisher had used on me. There was a label attached, which I read out: 'To a girl who knows what position she should be in. Right now, Lucinda.'

I made a face and passed him the cane. He was grinning as I stood back and bent down, resting my hands on my knees, but he wasn't satisfied.

'Touch your toes, Lucinda, and brace your feet apart.'

Again I made a face, but I did as I was told, adopting the new position, which I knew full well would make an even ruder display of my rear view once my dress had been turned up.

Magnus gave a pleased nod at my obedience, but he was in no hurry, tapping the cane against the palm of his hand as he went on. 'Now then, this is sure to hurt, and we can't have you screaming, can we? Somebody might hear you and get the wrong impression. That's why I'm going to pop your panties in your mouth.'

'I don't have any panties on.'

'Ah, yes, I was forgetting your predilection for going about knickerless. We'll just have to improvise, won't we?'

He stepped close as he spoke, to haul up my dress. I closed my eyes in a blissful mix of shame and fear as my legs and bottom came bare, but he wasn't content with that, taking it right up under my armpits, and as he began to fiddle with my bra strap I realised what he was going to do.

'Yes, this will do. Not quite as effective as a pair of panties, perhaps, but good enough to keep you quiet.'

My bra came open and I felt the weight of my breasts change as they lolled forward. It was strapless and he soon had me out of it, my nipples stiffening to the cool air as the cups came free. I'd already opened my mouth, to have it crammed with material.

'Good girl.'

He'd made me take my own bra in my mouth, adding to my awful feelings as I held my position, near nude with my cunt and anus on show behind, waiting for a punishment I'd wished on myself. I could have cried.

'There, don't you look pretty. Now, shall we find out what happens to Peeping Thomasinas?'

I already knew, in my case. They get caned, and I screwed my eyes up in terrified apprehension as he laid the thin shaft across my bottom cheeks.

'Just the one stroke, Lucinda, for now.'

He lifted the cane, and with Magnus there were no sadistic games, but he was a great deal stronger than Juliette Fisher. I heard the swish and felt it hit, a sudden hard blow followed by an agonising sting, far more than I could cope with. My gag stifled my scream, but I couldn't stop myself from jumping up and snatching at my bottom, which now seemed to be on fire as the heat of the stroke set in. Magnus merely watched, cool and amused, as I jumped up and down on my toes with my tits jiggling and my fingers clutching at my burning bottom cheeks, but he wasn't unaffected. Before I'd even finished my silly little dance, he'd pulled down his zip to take out his cock and balls. I went straight to my knees as he sat down, to take him in my mouth and suck, my head full of humiliation not just for being made to suck cock for the man who'd beaten me, but because the last person to give him a blow job had been my own boss, another man, but I was as eager as ever.

After a moment he began to stroke my hair and talk to me. 'That's my girl, you have a nice suck to make yourself feel better. Now let me see, how many strokes of the cane do you deserve? Six of the best is traditional, isn't it, and you're nothing if not a traditional sort of girl. So let's call that one a warm-up stroke, just to show you what you're in for, and you'll get six next Saturday, here in the warehouse, seven o'clock sharp. Got that?'

I nodded on my mouthful of now erect cock.

Chapter Thirteen

I'd have made a great medieval nun. A few impure thoughts, a confession and I'd have been stripped naked and scourged in front of the other nuns, leaving me with a clear conscience and a nice warm bottom. Not that it was really like that, I don't suppose, but it's a nice thought.

My caning had much the same effect, only better, because I had the rest of the week for my sense of apprehension to build up, which ensured there was never a dull moment. It also placed Magnus very firmly in charge, but he was not the sort of man to try to take advantage of my sexuality. I'd known one, at university, who thought that just because I liked to grovel at his feet to suck his cock and lick his balls it made me his servant. He'd soon found out he was wrong.

Magnus wasn't like that at all, treating me like a lady most of the time, and like a wanton little slut when that was what I needed, which was perfect, while I could now enjoy my bisexuality openly, and his. We even called in on Charlie on the way to the restaurant, to explain the situation and show her the welt he'd made across my bottom. As with Magnus, I'd been a little worried that she'd expect me to herself, but then we'd already discovered that we couldn't really satisfy one another because our tastes were too much alike. We'd even invited her to come and watch me get the cane on the following Saturday, which had added a new and thrilling aspect to my self-inflicted predicament.

I was a little sorry not to have been able to come clean to Mr Scott, but on the whole it was for the best. As Magnus had pointed out, it was something intensely private, while it would have been hard to admit what I knew about him without revealing at least some of my own secrets. That sort of thing was best kept out of the work environment, especially in a stuffy old company like ours, but it's a small world and secrets are hard to keep, as I was about to discover.

* * *

Wednesday was relatively routine, although the prospect of my caning kept me in a state of constant low-level agitation, so that by the end of the day I was eager to misbehave, only to have Mr Scott keep me working on fiddling details of the Chinese deal until nearly seven o'clock. By then I was more hungry than anything, while I knew Magnus would have gone home. I thought of Charlie. I stepped out onto the main floor and was about to ring her when I realised I wasn't alone. Stacey was still at her desk on the far side of the room. I smiled and gave a friendly but noncommittal salute, but she immediately got up and started across the room.

'Hi, Lucinda. I'd thought you'd have knocked off long ago.'

'No. Mr Scott wanted me. I'm on permanent call.'

'That must be tough. I've just had to redo an entire requisition report. Do you fancy a drink?'

'Um ... yes, why not? Just let me shower and get changed.'

'OK. Half-an-hour? I'll be finished by then, I hope.'

'Make it three-quarters.'

I needed three-quarters, because, while I hadn't felt able to turn her down when we'd only just made friends, I badly needed to sort myself out first, and that had very little to do with showering or changing my clothes.

Morrison was sat in his usual place, and I was pleading with him even as I shrugged off my jacket and began to unfasten my blouse. 'You know I'm going to be caned, don't you, Morrison? Yes, you do, and you know how

I feel about that. You should, when you've punished me so often, but just for now, just this once, I need you to take pity on me.'

His gaze never so much as wavered and I went on as I struggled out of my skirt and slip. 'Please? I just need you to fuck me, that's all. Just a quick fuck, please? Yes, I know I'm a slut, but I am going to be caned, so I will get the punishment I deserve. Please?'

I was down to my underwear and he watched as I stripped, unfastening my bra and letting it fall to bare my breasts, then peeling off my stockings one by one as his glassy stare lingered on my legs, before turning my back in embarrassment as I pushed my panties down but making sure I bent forward just far enough to treat him to a glimpse of bare wet cunt. Still he failed to react, even as I crawled naked onto the bed.

'Please? Just fuck me, Morrison, that's all I need, a quick dirty fuck. Please!?'

There was no more time to mess about, while my own silly behaviour had pushed me to the point at which there was no going back. I dug into the drawer under my bed for my harness and quickly strapped it onto him, fitting the largest and my favourite of the three dildos. Now he'd changed his mind, at least to judge by the state of his cock, eight inches long and rock hard.

'Thank you, you're a sweetie really. This has got to be quick, so I'll go girl on top for once, bum to face so

I can get friction to my clitty. Yes, I know that's a liberty. I know I ought to be on my knees, but just this once.'

As I spoke, I placed him in the exact centre of the bed and mounted up. I was already soaking wet, and the big dildo slid up me easily, making me sigh as my cunt filled with thick hard rubber. It felt exquisite, and all the better for the way Morrison's fur was tickling my bare bottom. I gave a little wriggle, pushing myself down to make my cheeks spread across his belly, taking the dildo deeper still and letting his fur touch the sensitive skin around my anus.

'Oh, you dirty bear! That's right, tickle my bottom hole while you fuck me. This isn't going to take long at all.'

It wasn't. I turned the vibrator on, and as I bent forward a little I spread out my cunt on the firm wrinkly surface of his balls. That alone would have got me there in no time, but with my bottom pushed out I was in a fine position for a beating, while the vibrations were making the tickling sensation of his fur on my anus even nicer. As I squirmed my cunt against his balls, my pleasure was already rising towards orgasm, and I began to talk to him once more. 'That's good. That's nice. Yes, tease my bottom hole. Can you see between my cheeks? I bet you can, and the shaft of your cock in my cunt hole. What a dirty sight. What a dirty little bitch, and, oh, if only you could cane my poor bare bottom while you fuck me!'

131

I was there, riding his cock to wave after wave of ecstasy until I had to bite my lip to stop myself screaming before finally collapsing forward onto the bed. For a few long seconds, I just lay there, my bottom in the air, thinking of what a little slut I was and what ordinary girls missed out on, but I was supposed to be meeting one within half-an-hour or so and there was no time for reflection. I made for the shower, washed, towelled myself down and threw on a bra and a dress, leaving my knickers off again for sheer naughtiness.

A moment to collect up my work clothes and prop Morrison up against the pillows and I was ready. He was still wearing his dildo, but I still felt horny and was sure to need another fucking once I'd got home, especially after a few drinks. I'd let him have his way, nice and slow, with my hands cuffed behind my back, maybe even up my bottom, and on that happy thought I left the flat, taking care to double lock the door behind me.

Stacey was waiting for me on the main floor, still seated behind her computer, although I noticed she'd touched up her make-up and put on more of the spicy, faintly citrus scent she used. That gave me something to talk about and we discussed perfume as we took the lift down to ground level and crossed the plaza. I'd assumed we'd be going to the bar we'd visited before, but she steered me around the side of a different block to a place that looked as if it had been there for hundreds of years, although it couldn't have been more than twenty since it was built. There were alcoves, each separated from the next by partitions of dark wood and frosted glass, one of which she chose for us before going to the bar and returning with a chilled bottle and two glasses.

'This is cosy, isn't it? Hardly anybody comes here, not from the company.'

'I didn't even know it existed.'

'I like to explore. There are all sorts of amazing places around here, some from when it all used to be docks.'

I thought of the Wharfingers, Magnus's warehouse and the street which included the Pink Pussycat, amused by the contrast between Stacey's life and my own. She'd gone quiet while she poured the wine, and when she spoke again she'd gone back to the subject of perfume.

We drank, we talked and after a while I bought a second bottle, all the while with Stacey growing quieter and less sure of herself, until she became visibly nervous, twiddling the stem of her glass and staring at the yellow-green gleams in her wine, so that I couldn't help but wonder if she wanted to confide in me, no doubt on some tedious piece of office politics on which I might be able to bring influence to bear.

'What's the matter, Stacey?'

She took a swallow of wine before replying. 'Did you know that I was on a management course last year?'

'Yes. I handled the applications for Mr Scott.'

'It was a busy couple of weeks, a lot of work, a lot of networking, a lot of people copping off with each other.'

She was blushing, and she was clearly about to make a confession, but I hadn't been there so couldn't see what it had to do with me.

'Go on.'

'I – I got very drunk and I ended up in bed, not with a man, with another woman. I really want somebody to talk to, and seeing as you …'

She trailed off, red-faced with embarrassment, but no worse than me. I was astonished to learn that there was another side to her, but also wondering exactly what she knew and why she'd decided I was the right person to talk to.

'How do you mean?'

'Well, you know. You're a lesbian.'

'No I'm not!'

'Oh, come on, Lucinda, everybody knows! You've turned down all the hottest men in the office, most of them twice.'

'Yes, but … all right, as you're being so honest with me. I'm bisexual, but that's to stay between us.'

'Bisexual? Shouldn't you be one thing or the other?'

'Not necessarily. Don't you like men?'

'Yes, but nobody in particular. There's a woman I like, but it's awkward.'

A sudden suspicion hit me. She'd always been mean to me, but then so had Juliette Fisher until the fateful day I'd ended up over her knees and then on mine. I decided to test the water a little, although her main problem seemed to be accepting her own sexuality.

'Doesn't she like you?'

'Maybe. I don't know. But I couldn't be open about it. My family would disown me for a start. So, what, do you like men and women?'

'Yes, but it's difficult in the office, so I prefer to keep my personal life separate.'

'Oh.'

She sounded disappointed, which reinforced my suspicions. I didn't want to hurt her, and she was a colleague, but I couldn't help but think of all the times I'd fantasised over the thought of having sex with her. Common sense said to keep the conversation impersonal and let her down as gently as I could, but the wine was starting to get to me and she looked so big and so strong, just the sort of girl I like, and not so very different to Juliette. I forced myself to stick to the issue at hand, or what she was trying to pretend was the issue at hand.

'Look, I know it's difficult, but let me tell you a story, about myself and a girl called Juliette Fisher. She was a little older than me, very beautiful, very dark, a bit like you really. She …'

I paused, wondering how much I dared reveal, even

though she was confiding in me, especially when Juliette's way of expressing her love had been based on doing horrible things to me, and my response on enjoying the treatment. It was best to keep it simple.

'She wanted me, badly. I didn't really know what I was doing, at first, but it felt good and she taught me a lot, including that having feelings for other people of the same sex doesn't necessarily mean you're gay. It just means you love people as individuals, for who they are, not what they are.'

What she'd actually said was that I was a dirty little slut who'd do anything for anybody with the guts to give me a hot bottom, but to admit to it would only have confused matters, and probably made Stacey run screaming into the street. As it was, she was drinking in my words and I carried on with greater confidence. 'So there it is. You went to bed with another woman, and I hope you had fun. No harm done. As for your family – that's life, I'm afraid. Don't tell them. My parents would have multiple fits if they knew half the things I've done.'

She looked as if she was about to burst into tears, so I leaned forward to give her a hug, which she returned with surprising intensity before suddenly breaking away, her blush now a furious scarlet. 'Sorry, I shouldn't ...'

Nothing more needed to be said. I sat back, feeling unsure of myself. All I had to do was take control and we were going to end up in bed together, and she had been involved in my fantasies so many times I'd lost count. She was a work colleague, but a work colleague who shared a secret, and who plainly fancied me. Even if it all went horribly wrong, she would presumably keep quiet, while if I took her to bed I'd be able to kiss her, suckle at her lovely big breasts, lick her to ecstasy, maybe even persuade her to sit on my face to make me kiss her anus the way I'd imagined it so many times.

I took a firm hold on her hand. 'Come on. We're going.'

'Where?'

'My flat. And don't worry about security. Just tell them you've forgotten something.'

She came, as drunk and giggling as I was myself, back across the plaza and into our building, where we forced ourselves to behave sensibly for a moment as we passed Security. We stood stock still in the lift, determined not to misbehave under the beady eye of the CCTV, but the moment we reached the safety of my door I took her in my arms to share a long open-mouthed kiss that set the seal on what was about to happen between us. Once inside, we were more urgent still, pulling at our clothes to get each other stripped down in the hallway, and it was more than I could resist not to take one heavy breast in each hand as they came bare, to suckle at her nipples in a gesture I was hoping she'd realise meant that she could do with me as she pleased. She liked it anyway,

Lucy Salisbury

sighing with pleasure before I broke free to scamper into the bedroom, where Morrison sat exactly as I'd left him, and forgotten him, propped up against my pillows with eight inches of black rubber erection thrusting up from between his furry black thighs.

Chapter Fourteen

'What the hell is that?'

'Um … that's Morrison, my teddy bear.'

'Yeah, with an erection!'

'Well, yes … don't you have a vibrator?'

'Not like that! What are you like, Lucinda Salisbury!'

I was doing my best imitation of a Morello cherry and didn't answer.

Stacey walked over to the bed, picked up Morrison and touched his cock, before immediately jerking her fingers back. 'It's all sticky! Lucinda, you didn't? Not just before you came out with me?'

I hung my head, my gaze fixed firmly on the ground, maybe more ashamed of myself than at any other time in my life, which took some doing. Speaking was out of the question, but I managed a single feeble nod.

She continued to inspect the harness and dildo, her face working between disgust and delight, only to suddenly speak up. 'Why not? You're right. It doesn't hurt anybody, and I feel so turned on, but ... but all this stuff. And what's this?

She ducked down, to pull out the rest of my harness from the half-open drawer, her voice full of shock and what I sincerely hoped was mock disapproval as she went through the various pieces. 'More dildos? Handcuffs? And what's this for?'

She was holding up the head harness, her eyes wide and her mouth open as she made a horrified inspection of the double-ended dildo.

I forced myself to speak, mumbling an explanation. 'You – you put it on your head. The short cock thingy goes in your mouth while ...'

'It might go in *yours*, but it certainly doesn't go in *mine*! You dirty bitch, Lucinda!'

My knees gave way and I sank to the floor, because this time there was no mistaking the tone of her voice, or the implications of what she'd said. She was coming towards me, holding the cage.

'I know I'm going to regret this in the morning, but come on then, let's see what you look like.'

I couldn't have resisted if I'd wanted to, my arms hanging useless by my sides as she pulled the leather cage on over my head, forcing me to take the thick rubber cock into my mouth as she fastened the straps at the back of my neck. She still looked horrified, but she was giggling as she took hold of the bigger dildo, tugging on it as if she was tossing a man's cock.

'I see how it works. Oh, what the hell, you're not going to tell anybody, are you?'

Nor was she, especially as she'd begun to fiddle with the main strap-on harness, quickly depriving Morrison of his manhood and taking it over herself.

'I'm going to fuck you too, Lucinda. That's what I did to Jacqueline on the course. I fucked her with a big fat candle. And I felt so bad about it, and here you are, all the time, ten times worse! Now let's get you in these cuffs.'

I was already kneeling on the bed and quickly went down, pressing my face and breasts to the coverlet with my wrists crossed behind my back. She took hold, quickly fixing the cuffs in place and I was helpless, not just under her command but under her control, with my bum in the air and my cunt ready for fucking.

As she got behind me she spoke again. 'My, but we did make a mess of your bottom, didn't we? And what's this? Have you been whipped? You have, haven't you, and you've been given a bit of a spanking by the look of it. Are you OK with that, Lucy?'

Her voice was full of sympathy and concern and she'd

141

called me Lucy. I nodded urgently, praying she wouldn't break the moment by making a fuss over the state of my bottom. Her hand came forward and the gag had been eased a little way forward, allowing me to answer her as she spoke. 'What happened? Are you really OK?'

'Yes. I'm fine. I – I got spanked, that's all, and given a stroke of the cane.'

'What for?'

'For being naughty …'

'Seriously?'

'Sort of. I just like it, Stacey, now fuck me!'

She let go of my gag, which slapped back into my mouth, making my eyes pop even as the head of the fat rubber dildo was pressed to my cunt and up. Her hands found my hips, taking a firm hold in my flesh and she began to fuck me, pushing deep up my hole and easing the dildo right out before penetrating me once more, until I was squirming with reaction.

'This is fun! Oh, you are a dirty little bitch, Lucinda, you really are! What does this button do?'

I'd have screamed if I hadn't been gagged. She turned the vibrator on, full, sending a violent jolt through me, and her. I heard her cry, felt her press deep and she was grinding herself against my bottom, not even bothering to fuck in my hole as she pleasured herself and reaching orgasm in just seconds. The dildo slipped from my cunt and she was sighing in bliss as she sat back.

'That was good. That was lovely. If this is what girls get up to together, I want more. Come on.'

She took hold of the chain connecting my wrists and pressed the head of the dildo to my cunt again, quickly pulling herself into me. Once more her hands found my hips and she began to fuck me, more like a man would now, with short hard thrusts that made me jerk and shiver as the sensations ran through my body. I was going to come, if she only kept it up, but before I could get there she'd pulled out once more and I'd been rolled over onto my back.

I thought she was going to enter me again and spread my thighs to accommodate her, only to have her strip her harness off and throw one leg across my head to lower herself onto the dildo protruding from my mouth. It was an awful situation, every bit as uncomfortable and humiliating as I'd imagined, lying there helpless with my wrists cuffed behind my back as she rode me, with her boobs in her hands as she enjoyed the dildo inside her, talking all the while. 'Oh, now I see. Yes, that is nice, very nice, and you do look a picture. Oh, Lucy, I am so glad I spoke to you, you dirty, dirty little bitch. I could come again, so easily, so very easily …'

She broke off with a sigh and started to wriggle on the dildo. I could do nothing, pinned beneath her with my mouth full of rubber cock and my hands strapped tight behind my back, neither protest nor beg her to take pity on me, nor what I wanted most of all, which was to get my fingers to my sticky well-fucked cunt and bring myself off. She didn't realise, or she didn't care, as cruel as Juliette had ever been without even realising what she was doing as she squirmed and wriggled her way to a second orgasm, while my excitement and frustration rose higher and higher still, but when she finally climbed off she at least had the sense to realise how much she'd taken out of me.

'I expect this thing hurts after a while. Come on, let's get it off.'

It was all I could do to lift my head to let her get at the straps, and when the dildo was finally pulled free I was left gasping on the bed. Stacey was still straddled across my belly, her hot wet sex pressed to my skin as she spoke again, her voice suddenly less confident. 'Your turn then. What would you like me to do? I don't mind licking, if you like?'

'I – I like things done to me, cruel things, like being spanked, and given the cane. Juliette Fisher used to spank me, you see, and she caned me. This time ...'

I'd been going to tell her the truth, because talking about it was turning me on but I needed a rest, only to change my mind. It wasn't the moment to tell her about Marcus, or Charlie.

'This time, it was after the paintball match. You remember how I ran off into the woods? I'd got really muddy, my trousers were torn and my bottom was a mess, and I'd sat in a cowpat. I needed to clean up, and this old woman let me have a bath, but she caught me playing with myself and she spanked me.'

'You let her?'

'I – I wanted it, sort of, like you want girls but you feel bad about it too.'

She nodded and I carried on, embroidering my tale. 'I got it over her knee, in the nude, and when she'd finished she made me touch my toes and gave me a stroke of the cane, just one, but it hurt so much. And then I had to do corner-time, standing with my nose pressed to the wall and my bare red bum showing to the room. Juliette used to make me do corner-time too, in front of her friends.'

That at least was true, but Stacey was starting to look doubtful again and I went on quickly. 'What would you like to do? You can spank me if you like? My bruises aren't that bad, and it's a lot of fun.'

'I'm not sure I could. I don't want to hurt you.'

'You wouldn't hurt me, but just now, could you get off? I need to pee.'

'Oops, sorry.'

She climbed off, and I rolled over to let her undo my cuffs, only to be struck by a sudden mischievous thought. 'You're going to have to help me, Stacey, help me pee while I'm still in the cuffs.'

Her expression changed to surprise, but only for an instant. 'You are such a disgrace! What, do you want me to watch you pee?'

'If you like.'

She shook her head as if in despair at my behaviour, but she was already helping me to my feet. 'Come along then, you little disgrace, and maybe I will give you that spanking after all.'

I came, led by my arm into the bathroom and assisted into place on the loo. She stood back, her arms folded across her chest, looking down at me. I tried to relax, already deeply ashamed of myself for even suggesting such a thing. Then I'd let go, my pee squirting into the bowl beneath me as Stacey watched, embarrassed and fascinated all at the same time, to make me feel small and silly, exactly as I liked, while it had been far, far too long since I'd deliberately done it in front of another girl.

'Now you. Do it all down my front.'

'Lucinda!'

'Please? But undo me first. I want to come.'

'You ... you ...'

She couldn't find words for what I was, but she'd reached behind my back to undo my cuffs, freeing my hands, which went straight between my legs. I began to stroke myself, revelling in how naughty I was being and begging her to do it, even though I knew I'd make it anyway, for the sheer humiliation of asking something so dirty and getting refused.

'Please, Stacey? All over my front. All down my tits and over my cunt while I play with myself. Please!'

'Lucy, I ...'

'Please!'

I was sobbing, near to tears as I begged her to piss on me, and suddenly she'd come forward, to straddle my legs, pushing out her belly at my face. My mouth came wide, I heard her sigh of relief and she'd done it, full in my mouth as I rubbed at my cunt, masturbating furiously hard as her warm piddle ran out at the sides of my mouth and down over my breasts, soaking my belly and splashing on my busy fingers. It was going all over the floor too, in a rapidly spreading puddle, but I didn't care, too far gone to think of anything except the utter humiliation of being pissed on and the beautiful wicked girl who was doing it to me. The orgasm hit me, every muscle in my body going tight as everything I'd done and had done to me came together at once, and at the first glorious peak I swallowed, to deliberately fill my belly with my new girlfriend's hot piddle.

A second peak hit me at the thought of what I'd done, and a third, my fingers still rubbing between my thighs as my ecstasy slowly faded with the stream of warm pale fluid flowing from Stacey's sex. She was giggling, and so was I, both enjoying our dirty secret sin, but I wasn't quite finished. There was one last thing to do, something I'd wanted since I'd first met her.

'Turn around, darling. Stick out your bottom.'

She hesitated, but did it, pushing out her lovely full bottom to make her cheeks part a little and show off the sweetly turned lips of her cunt. I took hold of her cheeks, spread them to show off the rude little star between, puckered up my lips and kissed Stacey Atkinson's anus.

Chapter Fifteen

My first thought on waking up was that I'd disgraced myself, and as I rapidly came around I realised just how badly. Not only had I gone to bed with a colleague from work, which I'd promised myself time and again I'd never do, but it had been with another girl. That was only the start, very much the start.

I'd suckled her tits. I'd let her fuck me with a strap-on dildo, put me in bondage and ride my face. I'd told her I liked to be spanked and asked if she'd like to do it to me. I'd peed in front of her and begged her to do it in turn, all down my tits. Finally I'd kissed her bottom hole.

'Oh, Lucinda, what have you done?'

I turned my head, to find Morrison lying on the floor, staring up at me, his gaze more accusing than ever.

'Sorry. Oh, bugger! Stacey?'

'I'm in the loo.'

I got out of bed and padded into the bathroom, not even bothering to pull on my robe. She was also naked, and about to climb into the shower. We'd cleaned up the night before, giggling together as we crawled around on all fours to mop up the mess we'd made, before showering together and tumbling into bed for more sex, this time head to tail as we licked each other to ecstasy. My final memory was of her climbing off me with a long satisfied sigh to leave the ceiling spinning gently over my head until the combination of drink and exhaustion had finally got the better of me.

Now we shared a guilty embarrassed grin, but I spoke first. 'That was –'

'– lovely.'

'Lovely, but very, very naughty. You won't tell anybody, will you?'

'You have to be joking! I pissed all over you!'

'Thank you. Our secret then?'

'You better believe it, but … there'll be another time, won't there?'

I answered by kissing her, and the feel of her softness and power would have quickly had me back on my knees, only there was no time. She turned the shower on and I got in with her, both of us laughing together as we soaped each other down, and this time there was no holding back. I let my fingers slip between her thighs and hers went between mine, to play with each other as we kissed under the stream of hot water, until I went down, turning her around to bury my face between the cheeks of her bottom. She was sighing as I began to lick, attending to her anus before starting to tongue her properly, lapping faster and faster at her clit as she wriggled her bottom into my face.

My hand was already between my thighs, rubbing with the urgency of knowing we had only minutes to make it, but that was all we needed. She came, crying out my name as her climax hit her, and I immediately turned my attention back to her bottom hole, licking and probing at the tight little star with my face pushed firmly between her cheeks until I too had reached orgasm.

We came apart and finished washing each other before stepping out of the shower, and, with my immediate need satisfied and the water off, I said what I knew was necessary. 'Yes, there'll be another time, Stacey, but there's something you need to know. I'm seeing a man, a local importer called Magnus Brabant. We've only been out a couple of times, but he's quite special. On the other hand, it's an open relationship, of sorts, so if …'

I spread my hands in a hopeful gesture. She nodded, although she looked disappointed, and I went on. 'I want to be honest, that's all. Oh, and it was Magnus who gave me the cane, although the woman at the cottage did spank me. That was so nice, and I do hope you're going to do it too, but for the time being we need to work out how to get you downstairs without arousing anybody's suspicion.'

'Easy. We spent a little too long in the bar. I missed my last train and you kindly allowed me to sleep on your couch. If I was a man, everybody would assume we'd had sex, whether we had or not, but, because I'm a woman, nobody will suspect a thing.'

***

She was right. There were several people around the lift as we stepped out together, but nobody paid us more than cursory attention. Mr Scott plainly didn't know at all, and I was not about to enlighten him. He was also distracted by a new claim from his wife, which made it a busy day for me, but a fairly straightforward one as I was used to her little ways.

I saw Stacey several times during the day as I worked on various tasks around the office, but we were on our best behaviour, never sharing more than a quiet knowing smile.

Thursday was movie night for her and the other girls from the main floor, so I didn't have a chance to see her in the evening, or Magnus, so I walked over to the Pink Pussycat to see Charlie and choose something to wear for my caning. I wanted it to be something that Magnus would appreciate, and I always think it's important to dress correctly for a special occasion. For this I wanted an outfit I wouldn't normally be seen dead in, and would be thoroughly ashamed to have on even for punishment.

Charlie understood immediately and began to give me a tour of her stock. 'How about a saucy schoolgirl outfit? We've got tartan miniskirts and big panties in white, navy and bottle green.'

She was holding up a pleated skirt so short it wouldn't have covered my bottom at all, leaving my panties on show before I even bent over.

I shook my head. 'No. I wouldn't look like a schoolgirl. I'd look like a stripper.'

'That's true of most of our stuff, I'm afraid. How about something retro? Here's a fifties-style dress with petticoats and frilly knickers.'

The dress was blue and spotty, pretty but just not right.

Again I shook my head. 'It's not really me, or rather, it's not *not me* enough to work, if you see what I mean.'

'OK, if you want something that's very definitely not you, how about this little black and white maid's uniform? It's satin, or satin-look anyway.'

It was black and shiny, with a white trim and a little white apron, but like the school uniform it could never have passed for the real thing.

'No. I like the idea of being a servant, but it's not right. I need something that brings me right down to earth, so I really feel the shame when my skirts get turned up.'

'We're going about this the wrong way. Hang on.'

She took out her phone, and moved to the end of the shop so that I couldn't hear her conversation, looking up occasionally to glance at me with a critical eye. When the conversation was over, she was smiling, but she wouldn't tell me what was going on.

I soon found out, when another woman came into the shop holding three dresses on hangers. One caught my eye immediately, a truly beautiful creation in heavy blue silk and fine enough to wear at one of my father's receptions.

Charlie smiled and leaned close to whisper into my ear. 'Imagine that turned up onto your back and your knickers pulled down.'

***

She was right. It was perfect. In a school uniform or a maid's outfit, I'd have felt small even before the ritual of my punishment began, but in my new and beautiful ball gown I would look every inch a daughter of wealth and privilege, not at all the sort of girl who'd be touching her toes for a caning. I would look beautiful too, rather than merely sexy, and, while people would no doubt comment if I wore it in the street, they were hardly going to disapprove.

I'd tried it on in the shop and it needed a couple of adjustments, so I had it delivered to work on the Friday, successfully avoiding the attention of Mr Scott, who was sure to feel I was misusing the working day, but not the attention of Stacey, whose attitude was just the opposite.

'That's beautiful! Are you going somewhere special?'

She obviously wanted to know what was going on, and I'd already been considering the pros and cons of inviting her to watch me being caned. An audience was definitely a good thing, but while I was sure she'd enjoy the view I wasn't at all sure if she'd be able to cope with my pain. I hesitated before answering. 'Um ... sort of. Are you busy later?'

'I was going out for a drink, but ...'

There was no mistaking the implication of her unfinished sentence. We were right under the eye of a CCTV camera, so I gave her a chaste peck on one cheek before going on. 'Say you have to work late and you can come up to my flat for supper.'

She nodded and we went our separate ways, leaving me with a warm flush suffusing my skin. I was going to have to sound her out before inviting her and I already had a test in mind, one that was sure to spice up my evening, and hers.

The rest of the day seemed to last forever, but I finally found myself alone on the main floor but for Mr Scott, who was still in his office, and Stacey, who was sitting diligently at her computer. I'd spoken to Magnus earlier and knew exactly what Mr Scott was planning to do with his evening, making it extremely difficult to keep a straight face when he came over to the lifts.

'Good night, Miss Salisbury.'

'Good night, Mr Scott.'

He'd gone down rather than up to his own flat, and I was imagining him on his knees with Magnus's big pink cock in his mouth as Stacey came over. We took the lift up in silence and kissed as we reached my door, then again as soon as we were in my flat, more urgently, with Stacey's fingers going straight to the buttons of my blouse.

I kissed the tip of her nose and pulled back. 'Not yet, darling. I want to teach you something. How to spank me.'

'You and your spanking!'

'Be fair. I'll do anything you want.'

'OK, but you're a very bad girl. You do know that, don't you?'

'Yes, which is the perfect reason to spank me. Right, sit down. Lesson one, there are lots of good positions to put a girl in for a spanking: standing, or face down on the bed, bent over something or kneeling in a chair with her bottom stuck out, even rolled up on her back as if

156

she's having a nappy changed, but the classic is what we call OTK, or over the knee, like this.'

Stacey sat down on one of my kitchen chairs and I got into position, across her legs with my bottom lifted. She immediately gave me a pat on the seat of my skirt, which felt so good I was having trouble keeping my voice steady as I went on. 'OTK is traditional, which is always good, and there's nothing quite like it to reinforce the difference between us: me, the one being spanked, and you, the one doing the spanking. With me across your knees, that makes you everything strong, everything dominant, my superior in every way.'

'And what does it make you?'

'A spanked girl, which says it all. Lesson two, when a girl needs to be punished she forfeits her right to modesty, which is why you should always spank a girl on her bare bottom. Strip me then.'

I heard the catch in my own voice as I said it, and I closed my eyes in ecstasy as my smart blue office skirt was rolled slowly up around my hips to leave the seat of my panties on show. She gave me another pat, firmer than before, and told me I was naughty, then took a grip on the waistband of my knickers. 'These too?'

'Yes, definitely. Knickers should always come down for a spanking, Stacey.'

She peeled down my panties and I was bare behind, with my mouth open in pure bliss.

157

Lucy Salisbury

'That's right, and so nice. Bare means bare, Stacey, and it doesn't matter who sees what, so there's no reason to leave a girl's knickers up when she's going to be spanked, ever.'

'But surely it doesn't matter? Don't you feel sorry for yourself, with your bare bum stuck out like this? And I can see everything, believe me.'

'Yes, of course I care, and of course I feel sorry for myself, but nobody else cares. I'm going to be spanked so I've had my panties pulled down, pure and simple. Now spank me, Stacey, and don't mind how I react.'

She began to spank, just gently at first but quickly warming to her task. I was in heaven from the start, enjoying simply being bare over her knee with the cheeks of my bottom bouncing to her smacks. Stacey Atkinson, who I'd fantasised over so often, now my lover, and the perfect girl to give me my spankings.

She was enjoying herself too, and after a while she admitted it. 'This is fun. Are you sure you're OK? I'm not hurting you?'

'No. Do it harder if you like.'

Her giggle said it all as she began to spank me harder, to make my skin sting and my legs start to kick in my panties. My thighs had started to come open, and I could smell my own excitement, which meant she could too. I stuck up my bottom, letting my cheeks open and showing off my anus.

A Study in Shame

'Dirty girl! You deserve this.'

'Lesson three, Stacey. When you spank a girl, don't be surprised if she gets turned on. OK, I'm warm now, you can put me down, at least for a bit.'

She ignored me, save to take a firm grip on my waist and to spank harder still, until I began to kick in earnest and yelp to the pain of what had suddenly become a real spanking. It hurt, but I wasn't going to stop her and she was definitely invited to watch my caning. Finally, it stopped, by which time my bottom was ablaze and I was badly in need of a hug, and to be put on my knees. I was shaking as I climbed off her lap, but I didn't get up, instead kneeling on the floor in front of her with my hot red bottom stuck out as I opened my arms.

'Lesson four, always give a spanked girl a nice cuddle afterwards, then you can make her go down on your pussy to say thank you.'

I came into her arms, to kiss her mouth, cuddle up to her and nuzzle her breasts until she got the hint and pulled one out to feed her nipple into my mouth. She let me suckle for a while as she adjusted her skirt and pulled down her knickers, before taking me firmly by the hair to ease me lower and pull my head in between her legs.

Chapter Sixteen

It was time for my caning. Saturday had been unbearable, with my feelings slowly rising as the time drew closer and closer. I worried about how much it was going to hurt, whether I'd start to cry, if Stacey would be able to cope after all, if Magnus was going to fuck me when he was done and what the girls would think about that. Stacey had gone home after dinner and I was alone in the flat, with only Morrison for company. I knew what he thought, that the harder I got caned and the more I was humiliated the better, and of course he was right. He was always right, the voice of my true conscience.

I let him fuck me, mounted up on my bottom with the big dildo up my cunt, which gave me a wonderful orgasm, but it wasn't enough. What I needed was

Magnus, a good beating and then hard rude sex in front of the two girls, maybe with them too. The possibilities were superb, and I was praying everybody would get on, enjoying the show, and me. Just to think about it had me shaking, and I didn't bother to get dressed again once Morrison was done with me, but spent most of the day in the nude.

At four o'clock I began to get ready, depilating my bottom and cunt, showering, checking my legs and nails, all the little details I'd have attended to if I was going to a ball. I took plenty of time with my hair, combing it out then piling it onto the top of my head, with a sapphire clasp to keep it in place. My make-up took longer still, applied with loving care, until I was every inch a queen, as my mother would have described it, and, if the reason I was taking so much trouble would have horrified her, that was her fault for teaching me the meaning of shame.

I was duly grateful, as nothing, but nothing had given me so much pleasure over the years, and it looked as if the evening ahead was going to provide a deeper, more shameful experience than ever before. Looking at myself in the mirror really brought that home, immaculate and poised for all my nudity, until I turned around to expose my rear view with the now fading bruises betraying the fact that I'd been beaten for sex. Now it was going to happen again.

My drawers contained several sets of underwear I'd never worn, including a complete set in pale cream, all silk and lace; a bra with full round cups, knickers that hugged my bottom like a second skin, a broad six-strap suspender belt and fully fashioned stockings. I put it on item by item in front of the mirror, thinking of how each piece would be revealed as I was readied for punishment, my modesty and dignity slowly stripped away to leave me all boobs and bum and cunt.

The dress made the image stronger by far, providing a cool aloof beauty in stark contrast to what was about to happen to me. White silk shoes added the final touch, lifting me to an inch under six foot, so that I'd be as tall or taller than most men, although not Magnus, not by a very long way. A small clasp bag for my essentials and I was ready, with just enough time to ensure that I got to the warehouse at precisely seven o'clock.

Only Security saw me leave. I was sure I could feel the envy and lust in their eyes as they watched my retreating back, no doubt imagining how it would be to strip me out of my pretty dress and put me across the front desk for a good rough spit-roasting. They had no idea, and I couldn't resist turning to favour them with a quiet smile as I went through the doors. Outside, the night was cool and I picked up my pace as I crossed the plaza, my heels clicking on the flagstones.

The walk seemed to last forever, even though it was just

minutes, but at last I found myself pushing in at the warehouse door, where Magnus was standing in a space he'd
cleared among the pallets. He was in his overalls, a working
man to my princess, and in his hands he held the long
dark cane with which I was to be beaten. Charlie and
Stacey were there too, seated together on the couch that
normally occupied his office, each with a glass of wine in
her hand. They had music on, a Mozart piano concerto.

Magnus wasted no time, pointing at the very centre
of the cleared space, where he'd marked out two crosses
with yellow tape. 'Stand there, Lucinda.'

I obeyed, already blushing as I got into position,
looking up into his ice-blue eyes as he lifted my chin
under one finger.

'Six of the best, Lucinda, bare bottom.'

'Yes, sir.'

'Turn around and place your feet on the marks.'

Again I obeyed, despite having to turn my back to the
girls and set my legs well apart, which meant that once
my knickers were down they'd be able to see
everything.

Magnus waited until I was ready before speaking again.
'Touch your toes.'

I went down, grateful for all my years of ballet classes
as I bent forward to touch my extended fingers to the
points of my shoes with my back still arched to show
off my bottom. Magnus came behind me, to stroke my

bottom through my dress, just briefly but it was enough to send a powerful jolt of shame and excitement through my body. I thought he'd turn up my skirts, but he walked past and spoke again. 'We thought it would be amusing to have the girls help to get you ready. Charlie, perhaps if you'd be kind enough to turn Lucinda's dress up?'

Charlie got up and I closed my eyes to savour the sensation of having my beautiful dress lifted onto my back, first the skirt and then the petticoat beneath, to leave me with the full length of my stocking-clad legs on show as well as the seat of my expensive panties. Magnus gave a click of his tongue which might have indicated approval for my choice of underwear, or merely amusement for the display I was making of myself.

Charlie went back to the couch and I was given a moment to contemplate the indignity of my position before Magnus spoke again. 'Stacey, I believe Lucinda feels it appropriate to have her breasts bare when she's punished, if you would?'

Stacey came up in turn and I had to endure having my chest exposed, first the zip at the back of my dress opened a little way, then the front tugged down to show off my bra, and finally that too disarranged, to leave my breasts hanging bare and rounded beneath me. She even treated herself to a brief feel, stroking my nipples and pinching each erect before breaking off as Magnus gave a cough.

'Not yet, my dear. That part of her punishment comes later. Right, knickers down.'

He did it suddenly, taking hold of the waistband of my panties and tugging them smartly down over my cheeks. I gasped as my bottom came bare, the cool air on my cunt and anus removing any last doubt that all three of them could see every rude detail of my rear view. Again I was left to think about the position I was in as Magnus stepped to one side, addressing the girls. 'Think on this for a little please, young ladies. This is what happens to Peeping Thomasinas: they end up showing a great deal more than they saw themselves. Isn't that right, Lucinda?'

'Yes, sir.'

'Good, I'm glad you appreciate that, but, of course, it's only the start of your lesson.'

As he spoke, he laid the cane across the cheeks of my bottom. I winced, wondering what madness had allowed me to get myself into this awful situation, but I knew the answer: my own craving for shameful dirty sex. That didn't mean it wasn't going to hurt, far from it, and as Magnus lifted the cane from my bottom I was gritting my teeth, determined to take it well in front of the girls.

'You deserve this, Lucinda.'

I heard the swish as the cane came down, to bite into the flesh of my bottom and lay a line of fire across my cheeks. All my resolve to be dignified about being beaten vanished on the instant as I let out a screech of pain and jumped up, clutching my hurt bottom and dancing up and down on my toes in a desperate effort to dull the burning.

Stacey gave a little gasp of shock and Charlie was giggling, but Magnus merely waited until I'd got over myself before speaking once more. 'Back into position, Lucinda, and do try to take it like a lady.'

He touched the cane to my bottom once more even as I resumed my humiliating position and I found myself begging him to wait, only to be ignored and a second line of fire laid across my defenceless bottom cheeks. I tried to stop myself from jumping up but couldn't, adding to the pathetic display I was making of myself with another silly little dance, but forcing myself to touch my toes again without having to be told.

Magnus was trying to hide a grin as he stepped away, passing the cane to Charlie as he spoke. 'I thought it only fair that we each had a turn, two strokes apiece.'

I blew my breath out, relieved even as Charlie measured up her stroke across my bottom, sure she wouldn't be nearly as hard on me as Magnus. The cane lifted, I closed my eyes, and screamed louder than before as the cane came down not across my bottom, but across my thighs, with a searing pain far worse than when it had been applied to the proper target.

'Ow! You vicious little bitch!'

A Study in Shame

She was laughing as she spoke, and imitating my own voice. 'Such language, Lucinda, really!'

My answer was a heartfelt sob as I got back into position, but Magnus spoke up once more. 'She really is being rather noisy about this, music or no music.'

Charlie nodded and immediately reached up under the short denim skirt she was wearing, to lever off a pair of tarty red and black panties. I knew exactly where they were going and opened my mouth, already resigned to one more humiliation. She crammed in the panties, gagging me and filling my mouth with the taste of her sex. Only then did I realise that it would have been a good idea to ask her not to cane my thighs, but it was too late, the hard line of the wood already pressed across my cheeks.

'OK, Juicy Lucy, here's number four.'

I winced, but the cane landed plum across my bottom, and even though it hurt I managed to hold my position, only to provoke laughter from both girls.

Charlie spoke up. 'Don't you just love the way her tits jiggle? OK, she's all yours, Stacey.'

Stacey had already stood up to take the cane, but to my surprise Charlie didn't resume her place on the couch but sank to her knees in front of Magnus. He saw I was watching and gave me a happy grin as he freed his cock into her mouth, but Stacey was already measuring the cane up across my bottom and I barely knew how to

167

react anyway. I braced myself, closed my eyes and nearly went over on my face as the cane bit in across my cheeks just as hard as when Magnus had been wielding it, to leave me shaking my head in reaction and gulping in air through my mouthful of panty material.

'One to go, sweetie.'

I hung my head, ruefully watching my friend suck my man's cock as Stacey tapped the cane to my bottom. Magnus was nearly hard, and his eyes were fixed firmly on my rear view even as Charlie worked on his erection. The caning was nearly over, but I knew exactly where his cock was going once I was done, and it wasn't up the girl doing the sucking. I was going to be fucked in front of my friends, a thought that stayed firmly in my head even as Stacey lashed the cane down across my bottom.

The stroke was as hard as ever, and this time I made no effort to hide my feelings, clutching my bottom and jumping up and down, oblivious to the ridiculous way it made my tits bounce, and turning to face my tormentors as soon as I could get my body under control. All three of them looked thoroughly pleased with themselves, although it was a bit hard to tell with Charlie, who was now tugging on Magnus's fully erect cock while she licked at his balls. I spat out her panties and threw them at her head.

'Well? What now?'

Magnus pointed to the empty part of the couch. 'Kneel down, with your bottom well up. I'm going to fuck you.'

I obeyed, climbing into position for entry. My entire bottom was on fire, and my thighs, the six cane strokes stinging dreadfully and sending a burning heat to my cunt, which felt wet and ready. Magnus was no less aroused, as he detached himself gently from Charlie and came behind me, to press the head of his cock to my gaping hole. He pushed, my cunt filled with one long, even stroke, his hands closed on my hips and I was being fucked, with my friends looking on as he thrust himself into me.

Stacey had sat down again, right next to Charlie as there was no space further up, and even though I was being shoved into the sofa by Magnus I couldn't help but notice that their arms were quickly around each other's waist. I smiled, thinking of all the wonderful naughty fun we could have together and how wrong I'd been about Stacey, only for my mouth to come wide as Magnus pushed himself in as deep as he could get and held it there with his huge hands kneading the flesh of my bottom.

I thought he'd come, and twisted around to take him in my mouth so that I could suck his cock clean of my own juices as I brought myself to ecstasy, but when he pulled out it was to let his erection slide up between my cheeks, rubbing in my slit as he spoke to me, his voice hoarse and deep. 'Stay still, Lucinda. I've wanted to do this since the moment I met you.'

He pressed his cock to my anus. I realised he was going to try to bugger me and was babbling immediately. 'Oh, God, no, Magnus, I can't take it, and not in front of everybody, not up my bottom!'

I twisted around as Charlie gave a nervous giggle, to see her passing him a silvery tube with a label showing two muscular young men, one with his bottom stuck out towards the other. Magnus took it and I could only gape in horror, unable to resist what was about to be done to me even as the thick slippery lubricant was applied to my bottom hole. I was shaking my head, but I didn't mean it and they all knew that.

Both girls watched as Magnus once more pushed his erection to my now slippery bottom hole, which immediately began to open. I felt my ring spread to the pressure and my mouth had come wide in reaction and in raw awful shame as my boyfriend began to feed his erection slowly up my bottom in front of my two friends, first the head, then more, all the way in, until at last his balls were pressed to my empty cunt. For the first time in my life I was being buggered, properly, with the full length of a man's cock up my bottom, and it was bliss. Better still, I'd been caned first and it was part of the punishment, and done in front of witnesses, with Charlie and Stacey now clinging tight together as they watched me get my bottom fucked, as if scared that if they let go they'd be next.

My hand went back and I was masturbating as Magnus sodomised me, already dizzy with shame and ecstasy for the feel of his cock in my bottom hole and the very fact that I didn't have anything up my cunt. I'd barely touched myself before my ring began to tighten on his shaft, and as he started to get faster I realised we were going to come together. My climax hit and I was screaming, begging him to do me harder even as he pumped spunk up my bottom and thanking him for my punishment, the girls too, who were now kissing, in a babble of words that ended only when he finally pulled his erection free of my anus and thrust it deep into my open willing mouth. As both Stacey and Charlie squealed in mingled delight and disgust, I began to suck.

Magnus had barely finished coming and gave a long sigh before he spoke. 'Now you really ought to feel ashamed of yourself.'

I did, and it was perfect.

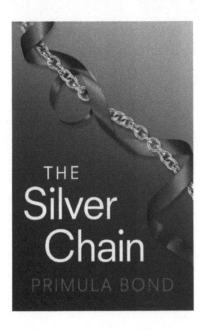

THE SILVER CHAIN – PRIMULA BOND

Good things come to those who wait…

After a chance meeting one evening, mysterious entrepreneur Gustav Levi and photographer Serena Folkes agree to a very special contract.

Gustav will launch Serena's photographic career at his gallery, but only if Serena agrees to become his companion.

To mark their agreement, Gustav gives Serena a bracelet and silver chain which binds them physically and symbolically. A sign that Serena is under Gustav's power.

As their passionate relationship intensifies, the silver chain pulls them closer together. But will Gustav's past tear them apart?

A passionate, unforgettable erotic romance for fans of *50 Shades of Grey* and Sylvia Day's *Crossfire Trilogy*.

GAME – JUSTINE ELYOT

The stakes are high, the game is on.

In this sequel to Justine Elyot's bestselling *On Demand*, Sophie discovers a whole ne'
world of daring sexual exploits.

Sophie's sexual tastes have always been a bit on the wild side – something her
boyfriend Lloyd has always loved about her.

But Sophie gives Lloyd every part of her body except her heart. To win all of her,
Lloyd challenges Sophie to live out her secret fantasies.

As the game intensifies, she experiments with all kinds of kinks and fetishes in a bid
understand what she really wants. But Lloyd feature in her final decision? Or will th
ultimate risk he takes drive her away from him?

Find out more at www.mischiefbooks.com

POWER PLAY – CHARLOTTE STEIN

Now she's the boss, everything that once seemed forbidden is possible…

Meet Eleanor Harding, a woman who loves to be in control and who puts Anastasia Steele in the shade.

When Eleanor is promoted, she loses two very important things: the heated relationship she had with her boss, and control over her own desires.

She finds herself suddenly craving something very different – and office junior, Ben, seems like just the sort of man to fulfil her needs. He's willing to show her all of the things she's been missing – namely, what it's like to be the one in charge.

Now all Eleanor has to do is decide…is Ben calling the kinky shots, or is she?

Find out more at www.mischiefbooks.com

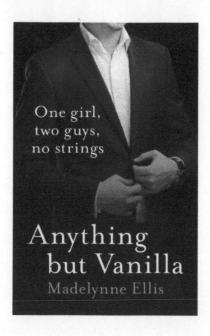

One girl,
two guys,
no strings

Anything
but Vanilla
Madelynne Ellis

ANYTHING BUT VANILLA
MADELYNNE ELLIS

One girl, two guys, no strings.

Kara North is on the run. Fleeing from her controlling fiancé and a wedding she ne
wanted, she accepts the chance offer of refuge on Liddell Island, where she soo
catches the eye of the island's owner, erotic photographer Ric Liddell.

But pleasure comes in more than one flavour when Zachary Blackwater, the charm
ice-cream vendor also takes an interest, and wants more than just a tumble in the s

When Kara learns that the two men have been unlikely lovers for years, she becon
obsessed with the idea of a threesome.

Soon Kara is wondering how she ever considered committing herself to just one m

Find out more at www.mischiefbooks.com